The
Short
Hall

Stonehenge
books

The Short Hall

New and selected stories by

James B. Hall

c. 1

Save one, these stories were printed originally in: *The Virginia Quarterly Review, Omni Magazine, The West Coast Review, Carleton Miscellaney, The Missouri Review, Atlantic, New Letters.*

BL JUL 29 '81

For Elizabeth Cushman Hall—
the woman I love.

By The Same Author:

v

Table of Contents

Introduction

Y ou are traveling somewhere you have never, never been before, and you are accompanying him. He is sometimes plural, but more usually a single male figure known as "I." You wonder who he is. Yes, he is perfectly willing to tell you who he is:

"Working as I do in Oakland for Blutcher & Son, Wholesale vegetables . . . as the auditor for B&S . . ."

"I accepted the challenge . . . for our ancestors, for a thousand years, had also worked these quarries, had climbed these escarpments of clay where dust and sky became one."

"Looking back on that instant of capture, I now wish the prisoner had tried to run. As a CI Captain, long in the field, I do not miss."

"I understood our Territorial Police mission in the midcontinent river basins. As I rose in rank from Constable to OC/OMT, I ran things by the Manual (as revised)."

These are identifications that, though perfectly plausible, you will soon refuse to accept. The stories are almost always ones of going somewhere, and you realize after a little while that your companion, "I," is proceeding by secret orders. He is not going just for the mundane reasons he professes to have, but there is an implant in his brain containing the Mission. You won't find out what it is—your fate is to follow him and to try to read the cipher of his behavior.

At the same time, you are quite unsure of just where you are. Oh, "I" will tell you that you are in an Ohio town that stands alongside a railroad; or that you are near Fremont, California; or that you are in a small mountain valley near a highway that leads into some unspecified town. There are never any landmarks. Sometimes there are familiar objects—buses, factories, or grain elevators—but seen

ix

en route to incongruous destinations. Is this a twenty-fifth century California? Is this a symbolical Ohio that gives way to the actuality of The Other Kingdom? Are "Oregon" or "Ochretown" simply signs, stuck up on the stage, that might as easily read "A Wood Near Athens"? Perhaps I should say that every territorial location in these stories is quite palpable and three dimensional but at the same time indeterminate and ambiguous.

And, in the same way, human action and reaction in these stories is often recognizable but incredible at the same time. In "Going North," an "I" is on a bus to Oregon with three men. En route, they stop in the night, go out into a snowy landscape, perform some strange suicide-rite (all except the "I") and freeze to death. "I," like many of the Hall characters I take to be real, has no graphics about him—or, no very specific ones. The three inarticulate men are minutely described as to hair, teeth, shoes, clothes, and body language—and I suppose that this realism suggests that they are not real. Or surreal as the doppelgangers of the "I."

What is "real" in any piece of fiction? To be honest, nothing at all, even in the most dogged attempts at photography. But all fictions are—like the planet in Nobokov's *Ada*—parallel worlds. We recognize them not because the small black sticks and curls on the paper bear any physical resemblance to a street, a house, or a human face but because there is an operation of cause-and-effect in the fiction that strikes us as much like the cause-and-effect of the life around us. But the beauty is that it's much more decisive; when princes fall, they really fall; when a hero triumphs, he really triumphs. Until Chekhov and his crowd came along, nothing was half-ass.

But we came to accept the modification of decisiveness, and even to take a pleasure in its shadings and equivocations. It still had many more outcomes per volume than a decade of growing older in the U.S.A.

But, passing on to what I believe is the inner mystery of James B. Hall's work, I think of a passage in Freud's *The Interpretation of Dreams*. He is talking about that oddest of fugues, the dream within a dream:

> As for the judgment which is often expressed during a dream: "Of course, it is only a dream," and the psychic force to which it may be ascribed . . . they are intended to depreciate the importance of what is

being dreamed. The interesting problem allied to this, as to what is meant if a certain content of the dream is characterized in the dream itself as having been 'dreamed' [is the fact that] that which the dreamer continues to dream after waking from 'the dream within a dream' is what the dream-wish desires to put in place of the obliterated reality. It may therefore be assumed that the part 'dreamed' contains the representation of reality, the real memory, while, on the other hand, the continued dream contains the representation of what the dreamer merely wishes. . . . In other words, when a particular incident is represented by the dream-work in a 'dream,' it signifies the strongest confirmation of the reality of this incident, the most emphatic *affirmation* of it.

In short, the dreamer lies to himself, but when the dreamer falls into a second, deeper state of sleep, he cannot avoid telling himself the truth. I think that standard, realistic fiction is usually the first, self-satisfying dream. The kind of fiction one finds in *The Great Wall of China,* or *The Diary of a Madman* (careful—this is a one-point comparison), or the kind of fiction Hall writes frequently is the second, internal dream, those truths the dreamer is powerless to warp or banish.

This is why Hall's fantastic stories are beyond fantasy in their apparatus. It is also why, for us startled readers tracking along behind the "I," the logic of why we are here in this story and what is occurring in it always seems to recede just beyond the horizon. We know it is there; all the other animals sense it, respond to it, but we can never see it, diagram it, or even learn to accumulate it, bit by bit. Of course, the dreamer—reader of fiction—does not understand his interior dream. He has to awake twofold before he can try.

It isn't my intention to try to "explain" the logic of any of the fantastic stories. The hard part, and the pleasure, is in your own twice-awakening—after which it comes clear.

My only warning is, don't mistake Hall's for all the debased dreams that are nowadays wrapped in ink and paper and shipped out by the ton. Of course, I am talking about the sort of general commercial category known as fantasy and science fiction. For the most part, these are small potions mixed by talentless dreamers. The mixture used to be very heavy in wish-fulfillment, but, in late years, has much more of the anxiety ingredient. But Freud, in the passage above, had identified them: dreamers who are incapable of falling asleep in the deeper dream of real-ness and, at the same time, incapable of awaking.

The best proof of this would be to look at any standard SF that is applying for some kind of Social Meaning and then to look at Hall's remarkable story, *My Work in California.* In it, the "I" is a tour guide who takes various groups of foreign specialists—Koreans, Japanese, Indians, Arabs, Swiss, for instance—to various sites of American symbolism. There is the Younger Factory, where infants are loomed in syntax; The Snow Orchestration, where winds create heroic, ancient images out of snow; and the Coma Pavilions, which has such curious features as The Matriarch Escarpment, a Cervix-Renewal and Depletion Station, a Meditation Pavilion for programmed faith loss, and Crucifixion Beach.

Instead of the bang-up plot-with-a-moral we'd have in a science fiction story or novel, Hall gives us a tour, noting every vision and every comment by the foreign observers, while insisting that none of this means anything to his "I." He is bored and a little depressed, looks forward to his vacation, where he hopes to meet someone interesting.

The only comparison I can think of to do this story honor is one with Charles Finney's magical (and now nearly-forgotten) novel, *The Circus of Dr. Lao.* Around 1935, in ordinary, everyday Abalone, Arizona, there appeared a most unusual circus, operated by a certain Chinese Dr. Lao. . . .

Of course, James B. Hall can also write first-rate realistic stories, of the kind he has been publishing for about thirty years. The ones in this volume are "The Rock Pool," "Foss," "The Executive Touch," and "Getting Married." Shrewd, well-written, dramatically-satisfying stories all of them—but I wonder whether they might not seem more at ease in another volume, or in a private section of this one, at least. After the fantastic stories, one feels the need of a psychological decompression-chamber, a chance to recover from the starshells and strobe lights. Not to step immediately out onto a sunlit suburban sidewalk.

Of these stories, all good, I'd suggest that "The Rock Pool" is the best. It's told from the point of view of two middle-aged peeping Toms, and it's the heartbreaking story of a beautiful boy and girl. Hall is very canny to control this by using the mundane curiosity of Mr. and Mrs. Emerson (the peeping-Toms) as a means of observing a sad, doomed, beautiful, young girl playing out the last few weeks of her life.

I suppose that any writer of prefaces is obliged to give some kind of overview, to try somehow to place the work in the context of contemporary writing. Hard to do, in this case. James B. Hall's stories would have been a literary sensation in the 20s and 30s, as highly original and unconventional work. They'd be in all the college anthologies today. But they come along in the twilight of the American short story, a time of fewer and fewer practicioners, a dwindling readership, declining publication. Katherine Anne Porter or Ernest Hemingway or any other good short story writers could publish initially today with small notice or acclaim. A dying art—even when it produces striking swan-song work—is not news.

All I can say to that is that the honest reader can forget all fads, fashions and trends and can read a book for the illumination of heart in it. Forget sales charts, New York reviews, book club choices, jacket blurbs by famous names, cocktail party comment—this book will never make it on those grounds.

But, with you, the reader, it has every chance to make it on the real grounds.

—Robie Macauley

The
Short
Hall

While Going North

Because his wife invited me to Oregon for Thanksgiving dinner "with all the trimmings," I knew my brother wanted to borrow more money for his sprinkler business (Rent Some Rain). Of course I had money because I work the Pay Window and use dock tickets to embezzle a certain amount for myself every Friday.

And that's why I claimed a window seat on the Express bus out of Oakland: to rethink my brother's wife, and Rent Some Rain, and those blue dock tickets—and when to stop embezzling. On that trip across the High Cascades, I really did resolve everything.

Actually, it was a long time after I looked back into the white-tiled interior of the bus terminal and after the bus paused at a signal and I saw the great lethal belt of automobile headlights moving overhead on the outbound freeway. Yet it was before I awoke suddenly and saw the moon balanced on a far rim of hills and saw a horse in the moonlight outlined against the wide, red lips of a woman's face on a cigarette billboard. Somewhere between—at Red Bluff or at Weed—three men appeared.

They sat down near me. They began to smoke bent hand-rolled cigarettes. When light from outside the bus flicked across their faces—first one, then another—I saw their hair was almost identical: overly long and probably red. They came aboard without any packages wrapped in newspapers, or even a suitcase, but they were also headed towards the High Cascades and to the wet green valley of the Willamette beyond.

At a comfort stop, I saw the three men clearly.

Past midnight the bus drifted through Chemult, where the store fronts in the moonlight seemed carved from lead; beyond the town the bus pulled off, and the tires on gravel made a noise like canvas

3

tearing. The restaurant was an imitation log cabin set in a grove of fir trees; wagon wheels of neon ran along the eaves and then became arrows pointing to the entrance door.

I was already through the cafeteria line and was re-reading a bus company brochure: "Thence to a comfort stop beyond Chemult (breakfast served!), then north across the High Cascades to Odell and Gold Lake, where the traveler may sometimes encounter seasonal precipitation falling as snow or gentle rain. . . ." The three men sat down at my table.

For the first time I thought of snow. You see, each man wore an identical summer-weight jacket, the collar open at the throat. Their red hair grew long in back, and down inside their unbuttoned collars. Their faces and their throats were the extraordinary white of mountain drifts. I recognized their common expression: leaving some place for good. Suddenly I felt a little bit ashamed; they had no money. They had been let out. I might have known.

Working as I do in Oakland for Blutcher & Son, Wholesale Vegetables, I see a great deal of "human nature." As the auditor for B & S, I work the window each Friday and therefore I see the faces of all the men who get paid off. To pay them off, we use blue tickets from our docks. I know the guilty look of men who are finished. To help them, I have a little street map printed on a card that shows the way to the State Unemployment Office.

Before I could speak, the bus driver was beside our table, a clipboard in his hand, a billed cap tilted back on his head as though he had been in the Men's Room throwing aspirin into his mouth.

"Everyone aboard, please. . . ."

I waited at the cash register while a sheep-faced country woman tried to figure my balance due from a twenty dollar bill.

"Well, one more time," the driver said, when the two of us walked across the ramp. I knew he felt the snow of the mountains in the wind; he was thinking of trucks jackknifed on curves, and of snow plows, their lights winking red against fir trees.

While I was still standing in the aisle of the bus, the driver abruptly turned out the lights and the wheels made the noise of canvas tearing as we rocked back on to the highway.

After my eyes adjusted to the dark, I saw they had shifted seats. Now they were beside me. In fact, I knew we were now traveling together.

Through my window, I saw the first roadside bank of snow. As

4

we went faster the night became the interlocked, chaotic branches of fir trees behind the white curve of guard rails.

Except for the three men and myself, all of the other passengers were already asleep.

Snow flakes turned to hot sparks in the headlight beams, then fled glowing past my eyes. Now banks of snow at the wood's edge covered the branches of trees and yet—through a notch in the forest, like a giant ledger suddenly opened—I saw windswept, iridescent meadows that seemed more distant than a star.

Because they had no packages in the rack overhead, the three men made no noise at all when they stood up. I, too, stood in the aisle and went with them towards the driver's tipped-back cap, a slant of black against the white square of the windshield.

At the summit, the bus slowed. Finally we stopped beside the Odell turn-off sign, barely visible in the roadside snow.

As I stood beside the bus, I saw the other passengers, their sleeping, half-lighted faces warm behind the windows. As I watched, the square windows moved past without a sound, and finally the tail lights were two animal eyes staring back at us in the dark . . . and were gone.

Only then, I thought of it: my suitcase was still on the bus, checked through; I seemed to glimpse it huge above tree tops, an apparition floating without sound, following the road down the pass towards the valley floor.

Where we walked, the banks of snow were higher than my eyes, and no cars passed. Overhead, the trees threw down chunks of snow when the wind tipped the fir branches.

Beyond the summit we stopped to breathe. Then, one at a time, we stepped through a notch in the bank of snow. I saw a causeway of snow stretching ahead in moonlight. In summer this had been a cleared fire-trail, but in winter we fell over logs buried beneath the drifts. Beyond this iridescent causeway lay Gold Lake.

For the first time, I felt the true nature of the cold. Even with an overcoat and hat and rubbers, I felt almost naked—but very clean. I felt very sorry for the men following in my own tracks. In their summer jackets, their open collars, and inside their side-lace Italian or Mexican low-cut shoes, I knew their flesh was turning blue in this blue wind.

By the lake, by the water's edge, I stopped. For a moment I thought the lake might tip sideways in the wind and cause us to slide along its edge and send us back to the highway towards the closed summer houses on the shores of Odell, or perhaps to some unknown club house, a place of much light where men hunted all day in the sun and towards nightfall sat before fire in a stone fireplace. But no, the lake was round and deep. The water was sullen. The light on the surface was like the reflections from white tiles inside a bus station. The indifferent eye of the lake stared upward from its socket of snow; this caused me to feel a strange warmth beneath my overcoat.

Behind me, I heard a voice. I saw the two men at the end of our line circle each other, arms held aloft like the overly long arms of statues. As they circled, they cried out; their voices were one voice; their words carried into the fir trees by the wind. Faster they moved. Each step packed the snow in an ever-widening circle. Then they were waist deep, still circling in the pit they had tramped with their own feet.

When I shouted, they slowly stopped. Each man held aloft one arm. With the other arm and hand, they foraged each other's clothing and pockets, throwing match covers and papers and at the last handfuls of coins up and out and into the snow. Their clothes were shreds. Beneath rags their skin was more purple than a tree shadow on snow.

Speaking no word, they stared at me for a long time. They turned. For a long time they looked into the surface of Gold Lake. Without a sound, they walked separately away. As I watched each man, without a sound, threw himself down in his own drift of snow.

Because their legs and arms were spread, the holes in the snow were the shape of cut-out paper dolls. I looked down into each man's face; I felt abandoned, left behind. It was the identical feeling of long ago when our mother gave my younger brother who now Rents Your Rain a party for his birthday, when the streamers of blue and gold and white made a canopy above an iced cake, when other boys and girls sang towards evening just before the rain threw itself in a tantrum against my window and stopped their voices singing in the living room, below the place they put me after one present burned in the fireplace. . . . The wind and the snow blowing turned each hole gradually into a mound; finally each mound was a shadow, a cut-out paper doll, fallen from great height into the drifts.

Then there was one man—and myself—beside Gold Lake. We

were alone.

I turned to this last man. The wind blew his overly long red hair back from his forehead, as though while standing immobile he was also running at great speed. Little sickle shapes of frost gleamed both from the buttons on his jacket and from the small white pouches of hoar frost beneath his eyes. As I watched the crossed buck-teeth became larger for cold drew back the lips with great force until there was an exaggerated, blue-gummed smile.

Knee deep in snow beside the lake, we faced each other. I felt a terrible intimacy, the kind the last two persons on earth might feel at the moment the last fire on some other continent flares once and dies. And also, from timepast, I sensed all of the other men who had come here—perhaps on foot or at hunt— and who were now beneath these drifts, row upon row, trying even now to rise.

His arms raised.

My impulse was to raise both my arms, to touch the palms of our hands, to remain in that intimate, yet wonderfully rigid position until the cold turned our touching bodies into infallible, glistening obsidian.

Yet because of a personal even terrifying will power, something I had always known was my own salvation, I felt that moment form like a cloud of white breath, then dissappear into the wind.

Because that moment passed, because I willed it so, I observed him dispassionately. I saw he possessed neither overcoat nor snap-brim hat nor overshoes—nothing, really, at all.

I struck him, and he fell.

Of course I tried to raise him, but his weight was too much. When his legs lashed out at me, his hole became deeper than ever. Each movement of his legs and arms caused him to sink, as though going down into the fir-green depths of the lake. Finally, in a single perverse gesture, he straightened both legs, was still.

By the early light, I bent beside his barrow of snow. I looked for a long time into his face. The skin was white. The eyes were wide and sightless behind frost. The overly long hair blew upward, as a flame might rise for a moment, and then it too lay frozen on snow.

I began to run in circles. I ran in identical tracks until the snow gave way beneath my feet, until I almost foundered. Even so, I circled each of the three mounds which had become three giant, spread-out snowmen.

In the center of the three mounds, I stopped all motion. I laughed.

I knew this much was true: my overcoat, my brown, belted, button-up overcoat, my snap-brim hat, my overshoes—in fact all of my clothes—layer upon layer of cloth and leather straps and bands of rubber—all of it had saved me. For this—mutely—I gave thanks.

As it does in the mountains, abruptly, the sun came up.

I watched as the lake became a sheet of orange light. The blue shadows of tree trunks went across the snow, a thousand small animals running.

Alone, I walked back along the snow-deep fire-trail, using my own footsteps as my guide.

Past daybreak I stepped through the notch in the snowbank and waited in sunshine beside the packed, cleared highway that led west through a tunnel, and finally into the valley where the branches of evergreen trees hummed in a green, moist wind.

In the town where they lived my brother's wife gaily waved as I came out of the bus station. Cec had been there earlier to meet an Express bus, but she, herself, blamed my late arrival on the goddamned holiday traffic all the way south to Cal-i-forn-ia.

And I said, sure enough. I knew what she meant all right.

Cec embraced me overly long before strangers.

After she embraced me again she said my brother was all tied up Renting Some Rain this afternoon until very late; so just the two of us could go to their place, to a two-bedroom apartment where as Cec said, she had "All them old trimmings."

We drank sherry in the kitchen. And that was all right in technicolor, and also in spades, and then it was "someone in the kitchen with Dinah, someone in the kitchen I know"—with all *them* ole trimmings—until Cec-baby winked at me and took me by the hand and led me into their new spare bedroom as I had hoped she would do when I first got aboard the bus in Oakland, when I looked back once and saw white light reflected on the white tiles inside the waiting room.

I had not thought her hair could be so auburn, spread out like that against the pillow.

I really did resolve everything: after the big dinner, but before I got on an Express bus headed south, with no hope at all of any repayment, ever, I loaned them both another four thousand dollars in cash.

Yes. And more where that came from, Buddy, as long as B & S pays off men at the dock with blue tickets—if you see what I mean.

8

My brother deliberately left the two of us alone for three minutes at the but station. After Cecy-O gave me a real big goodbye kiss, I said, "Well, we sure had all the trimmings."

"That," she said, "is what you think."

Because they now have a small, extra bedroom I know they will invite me back for Christmas. But next time going north, I'll no doubt fly.

And that's how I resolved everything.

Valley of the Kilns

I n these mountains, our flight together now past, I understand more clearly a return to the valley of my youth and to its factories might signify reconciliation and might be even wise; yet, against that compromise, I face again the ultimate fact of my wife now dead, and also two children. A sentimental gesture of return to the quarries can only dishonor love's memory. In this cave, therefore, I shall remain and here I shall die.

Before the death by falling (boy), by deadfall (girl), or her death (broken heart), I understood only a little the price of our rebellion. What I had not fully understood until now is how little our crime changed even slightly the established quotas of work, or the products of clay which at this moment are being fired, tallied, and cooled each week and each quarter of every year. In the Valley of the Kilns our names are not recorded.

To the thousands of workers who remain, our flight so long ago signifies nothing. No person shall profit from either our hardships or from the example of our devotion to one another. Were I to return to the Valley for trial, would public confession of error perpetuate her memory? I doubt it.

Nevertheless, I shall make this chronicle of two lives accurate with neither apology nor self-delusion intended. And as I set down these words which never shall be read, farther back in this cave I hear the great clay heart of the world beating darkly among stalactites.

At dawn, when the snowfields above wink in the first light, I foresee clearly my own fate: extinction by wolves when I can no longer walk our cave-path to the grove of oaks for fuel. Until then I accept austerely the seasons remaining. Toward evening, I watch deer walk from the forest near my deadfalls to drink; at times, when the rains of winter come my certain end may seem almost just. If by chance, in the future, someone reads these mere words on paper, no doubt they will make other judgments: each reader for himself alone.

Although in the Valley the routine of each morning is the same, I recollect vividly my first day of duty on the high escarpments.

Before the first rays of the sun illuminated the peaks, I was awake. In the farthest reaches of our barracks-caves, I heard hundreds of workers stirring, on their feet now, coming towards the light to work. Outside, the first "music" from the loudspeakers flooded our flat, wide, white assembly area.

Across the Plaza, on the front porches of their individual dwellings, precisely at the same moment, our foremen appeared. In a stately way, all in a line, they walked across the Plaza.

As the sun rose, all crews stood precisely at attention.

Fascinated, we listened to the roll call of production units; then yesterday's work done, and this new day's communal goals. With great excitement each morning I heard the tonnage for Escarpment-Six. With one voice we pledged Fidelity to the Kilns: our work to be pure, to uphold the customs of our craft, to sacrifice, etc., etc. My voice with a thousand other voices reechoed our pledges upward into the sun's first rays. And I was young.

Therefore I accepted with pride the challenge of the high escarpment, where the clay was talcum white. From those heights our kilns seemed only row-upon-row of brown-smoke hives no larger than a wineskin. We tamped black powder into holes drilled by hand. We blasted away great avalanches of rock which fell like a long white feather of rolling thunder towards the conveyor gangs three thousand feet below.

Our work was elite work. We knew the entire enterprise of the Valley rested upon us: without clay all kilns must cease production. The risk was great and only those with a nimble, extraordinary sense of possible catastrophe survived. On the high escarpments my character was formed, and I became a man.

Towards noon our Foreman signaled his drill crews strung out along the sheer, rising walls. Casually, we came down to his assembly area to eat and to rest for the one hour allotted to us each day.

"So: my eagles come for food?" our Foreman always said, and each day smiled at his own joke. Yet it was true; we called one another "Eagle." Because of rains or wind erosion, if an apparently solid path gave way suddenly with a hollow rush of air beneath a man's feet, we believed that man flew through space for a long time before the rolling, white-feather avalanche took him.

I saw two hundred men "fly" briefly, then disappear into tons of rock and white clay at our escarpment's base, yet not one man cried out. Instead, backs arched, arms extended and in that classic position they fell—down, down, became smaller, smaller—and at last tumbled end-over-end when the avalanche of rock took them.

Our bread, our white cheese, our customary wineskins passed from the eldest to the youngest man in our crew; vividly I remember the shapes of our brown, hairy legs as we rested beneath the shade of an overhang. Against the talcum-dust our feet were sturdily splayed, for our ancestors for a thousands years had also worked these quarries, had climbed these escarpments of clay where dust and sky became one.

At those moments of rest even a piece of bread became alive in the callous grace of our hands. Against white clay our intricately woven, encoded loin cloths breathed in the light; into our loin cloths were woven our future assignments, our destiny in the enterprise of the kilns. Only foremen and upper-level management could read those secrets; all others obsessively stared without comprehension. Besides our identical matching headbands, each man had a device implanted in the upper arm. At certain hours these devices made "music"; at others, especially at night, they merely hummed and we knew happily that something was listening.

When the sun setting touched the first rim of the mountains, we re-formed on a lower terrace; by now our bodies had become liquid-ivory statues, breathing easily. Sometimes singing, incredibly white from the blown dust, we went at a half-trot to the valley floor.

At the assembly plaza, later, especially in the windless nights of Spring, the kilns seemed to become upright, mighty organ pipes, glowing in their own heat, turning orange, then red, and just before dawn, pale blue. At those moments our singing became one voice rising from the dark, open throat of the Valley.

A feeling of right order came upon us. We were at one with an enterprise which signified purpose, something essential to our larger world.

One summer night exactly like that I lay half-asleep at the entrance of our barrack-cave. Above the escarpments I watched our constellation take more perfect shape: the Great Jug with three handles; to the West, The Brick, also mighty in orbit against the vast, ultimate furnace of our universe.

"Awake?" and it was my Foreman from the escarpment, his profile a blade of cast bronze against the light of our kilns.

"My Eaglet much awake?" his tone was ironical, the customary speech of all Foremen. In the mysterious way of management, he knew where to find me, and that I was awake, staring at our constellations.

Casually the Foreman picked up the end of my loin cloth. By holding it parallel, he shifted those patterns alongside the beads of my headband. When aligned, the two narrow sashes caught the light from the kilns, blinked, and for a moment, seemed to join to become one larger pattern.

"What I see here . . . Eaglet—" My Foreman then held the bead patterns unnaturally close to his hooked nose. He said, "Yes, . . ." and again cleared his throat.

Is . . ."

For the first time, I realized the man who had first led me to the escarpments was near-sighted; worse, his hesitation conveyed absolutely that he did not clearly read—could only guess—what my loin cloth and headband patterns foretold. With more of a shock than I realized at the moment, I understood the knowledge of all Foremen—and by extension all Management—was approximation, myth. Furthermore, in his moments of hesitation, my Foreman seemed incredibly old.

"Cert-ain-ly!" and I heard false enthusiasm. "She reads, 'new assignment'. Hah?"

Because I had grown to full manhood on the escarpments and had survived, I expected change; yes, and also reward and recognition. Yet because I had been taught so, at that moment I *felt* nothing at all. Thus my deeply protective reply was very much the tone of my Foreman.

"So: tomorrow is my time?"

Abruptly, he turned from me.

First he seemed an abnormally tall figure, his shadow massive, blue; then he was only a man growing smaller as he walked almost furtively back across the shimmering, absolute stones of the Plaza.

Because he had told me nothing, I called out.

He did not turn back.

Without thinking, I trotted across the Plaza, towards him and the first row of little houses where the Foremen lived with their "wives." I touched his shoulder.

Startled, he drew back. Fear was what I saw in his face, and in the gesture of his upraised arm. I had crossed their Plaza, had touched him. Because of my audacity, he drew back.

"Am I a Foreman?" I asked, "with house?"

He stepped back to the front steps of what might be his own "home." Because all windows in all the small houses were dark, I thought, *Why no one at all lives here. These are only house fronts. These doors lead only to other quarters, perhaps into barracks-caves.*

Far down the production lines an extraordinary flash of blue light illuminated his face, the house fronts, and his door.

"You . . . you have done well."

"Then a wife assigned?"

Harshly, in the dialect of all Management, he both spoke, and turned from me.

With one futile disengaging motion of arm and shoulder, he disappeared through the door.

And of course I never saw him again.

Bent low, I trotted back across the Plaza to the place where I belonged. If anything, I felt bereaved, desolate, as though suddenly on some high, rotting escarpment I had become afraid. As I reached the safety of our barrack-cave, the devide in my arm began to play softly: music for marching, and also music for sleeping.

I awoke beside Kiln 82-B.

That is to say, I came to understanding through work on our production lines. My loin-cloth patterns took me not to a small, white Foreman's house but to three years and 40 days as lead-off man beside the fire doors.

Past daybreak one day in spring our crew of men entered the firing shed; at the same moment, the crew-women also arrived through their portal.

Our procedure was exact. Each man of our crew placed carefully one molded, white-square of clay on the firing rack. The women opposite scribed the day's pattern and "fed" the clay with a brush and red-vitreous glaze. Whereupon Caliper-men thoughtfully measured each brick and each row of bricks, trying without rancor to find their own quota of "Second-Forms." Nimbly, within the permitted time-frame, tier-upon-tier the pallets rose as high as our tallest man could reach. For the firing run all pallets required perfect alignment.

The Talley-men, those roving jackals with clipboard and abacus, came and went; our Foreman with his symbolic, lashless whip of porcelain stood high above on his platform, never smiling.

Beyond my lead-off station, always, I was aware of the curved door of our furnace and of the fires within. At a signal from the platform above, I rolled back our furnace doors. One crew on either side, together, we pushed forward the wheeled truck of perfectly aligned, unfired bricks. When the heat caused the others to fall back, I, alone, pushed the load deeper into the furnace. Then I, too, was outside, and the door of the kiln slammed shut, then locked.

At once we walked all in a row to the rear of that somberly roaring kiln. We pulled forth an incandescent, square honeycomb of new bricks which glowed among us like the sun.

To see an aligned, glowing dolly of bricks emerge triumphant from its weeklong fire made us cry out in an almost indescribable joy. As we watched, still another crew pushed that truck—glowing steadily, turning red—towards cooling yards. Always we watched the square of light grow smaller until it was only a firefly disappearing. Outside everything was dark as pitch.

At such a moment we met.

To "meet," however, implies special circumstance. To be sure I had seen her each day for almost three years, but precisely because each worker inexorably was at one with our production, with the ideology of our Valley, the distinctions between men and women, while on the production lines, long ago had ceased to exist. With that distinction vanished, we spoke to one another only in quota-words, or by communal song. Thus to see another person or to touch accidently across a pallet of clay was not at all to "meet."

As had happened before, exactly when the last pallet of the day emerged from our kiln, I had a terrible moment of vision. Three times before when I looked into the flames, unmistakebly I saw my own face. That day, however, writhing, as though sculptured in flame, I saw the outline of my whole body, complete with loin-cloth patterns.

Blind, stricken, I fell down in the monstrous blue shadow of our Whip's platform. For one moment he too was blinded by the fiery sun of new bricks emerging.

"You do . . ." was what she said very softly, her face partly averted, "More . . ."

What she said was illicit, and also not possible—that *anyone* could do "more"; yet secretly, I knew in my own heart what she dared say was true.

"More than anyone . . ."

The movements of my body had told her so: at the furnace door, then deeper into the flames than anyone else, I dared push our pallets; on the production line, at times, I was an Eagle still, high on the escarpment's most daring walls. And this, secretly, she had understood. As it had been so very long ago when I had seen a Foreman's profile against blue light, so was it with her at that moment: her profile against the kiln's subdued, overhead glow, her lips half-open.

We did not touch.

Instead, impulsively, she picked up the end of my loin cloth. Intently, her face without expression, she held the pattern of her loin cloth in parallel to mine. Never before had I seen a woman's hand do something so intensely feminine.

In the shadow of the platform above, at a moment when even the Talley-men were blinded, on shards of old brick, illicitly and contrary to Law and in the face of death by burning, she kissed me.

Terror was what I felt, and the Valley suddenly seemed to tremble because of our unplanned disobedience. Then as though we had passed only in those shadows, we stood apart, stepped back into our respective lines.

In the next weeks, two things happened.

At Kiln 82-B my personal effort—a concept not before known to me—redoubled. I sensed new, illicit purpose. I pushed our piled-high carts of unfired bricks almost into the very heart of the awful flames. Secondly, in ways I had not thought possible, she managed to put glaze on almost every brick which I placed on any pallet. No word was spoken, yet our work seemed to be for ourselves alone. And it was true: she managed to let others place her just beyond my touch, and yet I could observe her closely.

Of course we had no names, and outwardly she was precisely as all other women I had ever seen except in the center of her black, long hair was an enigmatic skein of ash-white. When the heat of the kiln blew her hair back across her shoulders, that line of color

17

glowed and floated as I watched. Clearly that mark was her disqualification to bear children. Furthermore, I saw now a destructive, impulsive aspect of her work. She was wasteful of glaze, and at day's end impulsively threw down the honored tools of her craft. But would she, ever, see her own face in the consuming flame? I could not know the answer.

After six weeks we met again in the darkness beneath a Talleyman's decorated platform, our feet bare on shards of brick.

With absolute disdain for the symbolic porcelain whip above us, she said, "Tomorrow, I go down . . . to the cedar forests."

Terror was what I felt. Even with the Talley-man directly overhead I might have cried out but she touched me, placed her blunt, short fingers across my lips.

Far down the tracks towards the cooling sheds, we saw our last dolly of bricks glowing, becoming smaller in the exceptional, somehow comforting, darkness.

Without saying anything, she turned towards the receding light, and because of love for her I took the second step. We were two shadows running, following the narrow rails onward. Then we were going underneath vast, half submerged sheds, their roofs held up by massive columns of brick.

Suddenly, ahead, the glowing, honeycomb of fired bricks flared, went out: the tracks had abruptly turned. Because it was totally dark, we walked more slowly. Underfoot were shards of pottery, of brick; overhead we saw massive savagely decorated platforms where once Foremen and Talley-men austerely watched. These platforms from another age were now impotent, deserted, were falling down.

Beside a low, final tower we emerged beneath the sky and climbed the roughhewn, primal steps to an upper platform. Stretched out ahead in the moonlight, humped like the back of some sleeping, vicious animal, I saw the roof of cooling sheds stretching away.

In full flight, with no guide save the escarpment to the East, gradually we went towards the docks, the shipping yards. On either side we passed between pallets of stacked-up bricks with three holes, then past canted stacks of jugs in a hundred sizes, all with three handles. Gradually these piles became smaller, the sheds more haphazard. After four miles, the shed roofs were rotted, or blown away, the abandoned roof posts no taller than my waist. At last even the posts were only piles of rubble, covered by silt or by clay blown here by the winds . . .

On a rise of ground beyond the vast vestige of those mounds, at two o'clock in the morning, we stopped. For a moment we turned, looked back. Beneath the sky we saw blue and orange organ pipes of flame, a mosaic of streets and plazas, the row-upon-row of mighty kilns, the entire Valley a hearth glowing—the place where we were born. Ahead was only a canyon of stone, a prelude to the chaos of mountains.

Listening intently, we heard for the last time the far-off, sweet, industrial hum rising from the Valley of the Kilns. We felt bereft, but we did not turn back. What I saw next made all of the difference.

When we fled the kilns, I feared the areas of the yards, and the river docks. Here the Talley-men roved with their giant, three-eyed dogs. These areas were central to our enterprise, to our dogma: our crews in the forest, on the escarpment, beside the kilns, or in the vast network of cooling sheds; yes, and our myriad of quotas, our athletic games when we ran long distances carrying heavy weights, and most especially the patterns programmed into our loin cloths.

This we believed: from our yards and docks—made Holy by Shardsmen—our tile and our brick moved onward to construct walls and fantastic cities high on mountain tops we had never seen. These things known were the end, the justification of all our sacrifice.

Yet here, beyond the most savage, burnt-out cooling sheds, there were no railway yards. No docks. Where rail yards might have been, I saw only ancient, low ridges coming together. These ridges intersecting might once have been a primitive system of dikes, or canals, or possibly roadbeds—now abandoned, now overgrown.

What might have been rails, or steel shining, was only dew on ground-running tendrils reflecting the light of the moon, or reflecting the kiln-flames from the Valley itself. Beneath vines, beneath wind-blown gorse, I sensed there were only incredibly ancient rows of crude bricks which of their own weight and a thousand years of rain, were sinking inexorably into the earth from whence they came.

Stupefied, unable to speak, I sat down on a low turtle-shaped mound of pottery shards—said nothing at all. As in a moment of vision, all the things heretofore not known or taken on faith in all my life seemed suddenly to become clear. In that terrible moment, I came truly to light. I understood. After this knowledge there was no forgiveness.

I looked up. I intended to share with her my revelation.

In her face I saw something both significant and terrible. She was sitting erect, smiling. Her face in the moonlight was full of another kind of wonder, an expression I knew too well. Although she saw what I saw, her mind, her imagination, was different. She had never been on the high escarpments. Therefore I understood she did in fact see "railroad yards." She saw what she had to see: docks, barges, and long lines of freight cars rolling. Her faith was absolute; she had never seen her own face burning like a rose inside a kiln. Only because of me she had come here, because of love—and that was enough.

Perhaps we might have returned the way we came. With good fortune, I might have lived out life in the kilns, silent, an outcast because of my fatal knowledge, awaiting my final years as a toothless, muttering grader of shards. Perhaps her spirit really was the spirit of the cedar forests; perhaps there was Justice after all, in the pattern of our loin cloths . . .

But we did not turn back.

I pointed ahead to a low notch in a wall, and to the dark canyon of stone beyond.

With impulsive, almost childish glee, with her long, black hair blowing in the first wind of morning, she took my hand. She raised me to my feet. She laughed and I laughed and as we ran the longest journey of our life began.

The sun rose. As we paused for the last time to look back, far away and far below, I saw the high escarpments turn for one moment into flame.

The path leading always upward took us between flowers and across the first high-mountain meadow. There in a grove of sweet, low-growing pines for the first time, we made love and then slept in each other's arms until the sun was overhead.

The Rock Pool

The girl's sports car was a dust-covered animal running between the trees of the lane and then into their ranch yard. From behind the screen of the kitchen door, Mr. Emerson watched her car skid, and stop. Only then did the girl seem to realize the highway and the lane had come to an end so she turned off everything very quickly: her radio, the tape deck, the engine. As though it had caught up with her at last, a cloud of dust hunched above the car's hood, settled, and disappeared into the ranch yard clay.

Even after it was all over and largely forgotten by the neighbors, Mr. Emerson remembered for some years the day the girl first parked so abruptly: her unnaturally blond hair in contrast to the car's leatherette upholstery, the car itself a low daub of red against the upright, grey, side of the barn; how the girl allowed her shoulders to slump for a moment, as though to turn herself off, as though she was never going to drive anyplace again. And yet Mr. Emerson knew she could have seen only his wife's Cabin-for-Rent sign beside the Emerson mail-box three-quarters of a mile back towards the blacktop, county road.

"I would," Mrs. Emerson told the girl after they had walked through the cattle gate and had walked side-by-side down the arroyo to see it.

The cabin was very nice: one room only, a refrigerator beside a pre-fab shower stall; a kitchenette, all very nicely furnished, of course; a double bed, bookshelves built right into the walls, and nice closets for blankets—surely not needed in this weather—and also extra pillowcases and sheets. From the steps of the porch one nice view was up towards the farm gate, the big ranch house, the Petrolane tank and the waterpump enclosure screened by ferns;

then another nice view was down to the foot of the rock steps which led to the pool—a wide, bulldozed place, walled with stones, and fed by water diverted from the creek. As for neighbors, nothing except ferns and the valley which was giant receding terraces of redwood trees all the way to Santa Cruz.

"Would have to collect also a last-month's rent, in advance," and because to this girl the austere, shed-roofed cabin above the rock pool was a place of immediate, windless peace, she counted out ten-dollar bills and did not inquire about utilities, or a rent receipt, or guests, or who would wash the sheets when the time came.

And no: the girl would require no help from Mr. Emerson to unload the car; and no, would not accept a warm first-meal in the Emerson ranch house because in the car there were leftover things to eat in a cardboard box. Therefore the Emersons understood privacy was wanted, and complete independence from everything and everybody was the basic idea; and finally, no, there would be no real incoming mail, from anyplace, although it was nice to know the number of this Rural Route out of Santa Cruz.

While the Emersons ate strawberries from their own garden, they heard the first music from her car's tape deck, now transferred and hooked up inside the cabin, playing through her portable radio, playing very loud, very electronic guitar music.

At eleven, when Mr. and Mrs. Emerson were side-by-side, not touching or even thinking of anything like that, the girl's cassettes turned out the identical chords again and again. The sounds overflowed the cabin and filled the rock pool and the whole arroyo. As yet they did not in fact know her name.

"From San Francisco, heading south?"

"Judging by the dust, perhaps from New Mexico, by way of Bakersfield. Headed north."

"Or an airline stewardess? Let go for something . . .?

"I'm Sadie," Mr. Emerson said in a suggestive, "Fly me to Miami," and Mrs. Emerson said, "Huh!"

After a minute Mrs. Emerson said, "Well, I will visit her," for in most cases the Truth would come out.

Mr. Emerson almost said, "I'll take a look myself," but the implication was not good. This month he was fifty-nine years old and the wife was pretty much past doing much along *those* lines. He accepted it: now she pretty much dug in her own flower beds—

and that was that. Nevertheless, Mr. Emerson remembered precisely the inflamed, greedy moment he had offered to carry the girl's expensive suitcase into the cabin. Beside the opened trunk of her car he had sensed her fragility, her brittleness, and also a kind of desperation which was vulnerable and also inviting.

In a voice calculated to suggest this day was almost over, Mr. Emerson said, "I'll check her registration slip sometime. In the car."

"Well, that young lady came from *some*place. . ."

Abruptly, because their own front door might not be locked, Mr. Emerson got up. He walked through the familiar rooms to the side windows. Just then the lights of the cabin switched off; the music abruptly stopped. Through the windowpane he saw the straight edge of the cabin roof against a third-quarter moon above the arroyo. And wouldn't the girl be in the double bed, beneath clean sheets, with possibly nothing on at all, or however she slept?

After Mr. Emerson returned to their own queen-sized, childless bed he suppressed everything he had felt or had thought. Partly to avoid thinking at all about the girl and partly to divert any possible suspicions he said, "You were a smart woman. To work it out. Never honestly thought you would rent it. Away out here."

"There is always someone," Mrs. Emerson said, and again she felt justified, complete. The month-in-advance was also money in the bank no matter what might happen.

Then Mrs. Emerson turned once and gave herself to the marble landscapes of all sleep.

II

For ten days the girl lived alone in the rental cabin. Each morning and each afternoon on a ledge of rock she felt she healed herself by dozing in the sun or by staring at creek debris which by chance entered the pool, circled twice with the current, and then floated downstream over boulders.

Later, when they talked about the exact moment it began, the girl said she was not even surprised when higher up along a path the first two rocks dislodged and bounced down, and then she heard footsteps coming. When the girl looked up the man—a boy really—came out of the brush to the pool's edge. She knew at once he was hiking for he had a back-pack of blue and a matching canteen.

Later, when they talked about the exact moment it began, the boy recalled he had first seen the white Petrolane tank humped in ferns, and the cabin roof against the sky, and then—while looking across the pool for a path that might take him to a road—only then did he see the girl sunbathing on a shelf of rock.

What he wanted most was to fill the blue canteen, and of course the pool looked very pure but then pollutants were everywhere. . .

She felt the boy was probably three years younger—so would be just out of high school. And as it turned out, to celebrate graduation, his parents had sponsored this cross-country hike, a different, really outdoor way to see the West. That's why he was hiking south: had entered the woods just below San Francisco and had followed the earth's contours with a very detailed surveyor's map. When he traced the route until now, she saw he really had come in a beeline, and eventually would touch the coast just north of Monterey Bay.

David followed her along the cut-out stone steps to the cabin. There she ran water from the tap until they heard the pump of the engine begin to work in the ferns beside the Petrolane tank. When the water was cold he drank a very great deal and then he sat down on the floor his pack propped against the white stall of the shower.

Looking back on it a week later, they agreed it was almost exactly in this way that their relationship began.

III

After supper the Emersons sat on their front porch to watch the pelt-like shadows of evening take first the redwoods, and then the upper meadow, and finally the long valley towards Santa Cruz and the sea.

"That boy is somewhat younger," Mrs. Emerson said. On the pretense of delivering the rent receipt and also a calculated, above-criticism loaf of warm nut-and-raisin bread, she had visited the little house. At noon she saw the young man in blue bathing trunks stretched out big as life on the opposite side of the pool. "Also of some background and manners, if standing up for introduction to an older woman signifies. . ."

David was the first name. And in the present fashion, last name not stated.

Even in the darkness of their porch, however, Mrs. Emerson did not disclose her first, uncalculated reaction; for some years she had well understood how tolerant J.W. could be regarding the so-called private conduct of others. Yet she knew her first reaction was a fact and when she saw the two, separate, distinct growths of white flesh on the rock ledge above the water, she thought: what about later? And yet, instantly, that feeling gave way to a resentment. She knew her resentment was also a fact. She hated the casualness of it, the way they were lying not very far apart in the reverberating heat of the arroyo walls, with nothing better to do with themselves when she, herself, had been up since daylight, had already done a full day's work.

Actually Mrs. Emerson had paused beside the cabin porch to make certain it was not her imagination and then she called "Yoo-hoo" towards the blond young thing stretched out like a half-naked lizard on a rock, and then walked down the steps to deliver receipt and bread pan—and very naturally getting a closer look at them both.

"Thanks," the young woman said, and tucked the rent receipt between the bread loaf and the pan.

"This is David," and the young man smiled, and put out his hand.

If no last name revealed, probably this visit was temporary, so as yet no real chance to give the cabin a bad name.

There was an awkward bird-whistle and wind kind of silence. Because the boy was a little shy, and because the young woman seemed never to say anything at all, Mrs. Emerson said very cheerily, "See you two. Later."

As she turned, the young man called after her and she came back.

"Is it okay?" and David spoke very openly, very innocently. "If I rest here. Awhile?"

If the young woman felt anything at all, if she had prior knowledge of the question, if she actually heard the question, she gave no sign, no hint of any future involvement. The boy was asking this simply for himself.

"Why yes," Mrs. Emerson had to say with a hearty, country hospitality. And then when she saw other implications, she denied complicity, or even partial responsibility for anything that might come to pass. "That's entirely up. To—ah—to *her*."

Again the young woman neither replied nor changed expression, and so with a country woman's accommodation of both neighborliness and a kind of outrage almost entirely suppressed, Mrs. Emerson

25

turned up the stairs again and said back over her shoulder, "So long. You two."

Once through the ranch-yard gate, and out of sight, Mrs. Emerson changed dresses quickly. Then she went into the side yard and weeded and deep-hoed a flower bed which was not at all doing well for July.

Now, on the front porch, they could not see each other's face.

In silence they rocked, as was their habit. Towards bedtime Mr. Emerson recalled once more with absolute clarity what he, himself, had seen past noon.

Actually he had spent the morning with the back-pasture well. Then, upon return to the barn, he thought, Why not take a look at the rental cabin pump? So, since his hands were already greasy, he went there and that's why he had the toolbox open and the cover off the pump when the girl came out of the cabin.

The girl was lithe, and her buttocks were really mature and there was in her walk a movement, a thing which signaled looseness, a past history no doubt of at the right time doing—well, doing everything. . .

Halfway down the carved-out steps of stone, the girl finished tying her straps. From above, through ferns, Mr. Emerson saw the bed-sheet white of her breast—actually only half a breast. But he saw it. Just like that.

What he felt and what he wanted to feel was pure, and lustful, and entirely bestial, the way he always felt when he watched animals on the farm do the job—and then absolutely forgot what had just happened to them. It was a feeling he knew and a feeling he never denied to himself.

Deliberately, Mr. Emerson came back to business, to the pump. He placed one hand on the electric motor housing—warm; he touched the drive belt—good tension; the fifty-gallon tank—full. Only a drop of oil was needed, and also a half-turn of the grease cup on the main shaft. . .

When he looked down again through the parapet of ferns, the girl was sunning. Her hair lay windblown across the rock; her shoulders were no match at all for stone outcrop. Her legs were together—just now—but at the right time the position of the legs could be changed, could be spread out. . .

For some little time Mr. Emerson looked down through ferns to the pool below. Wrench in hand, immobile, without present or even any future hope of direct satisfaction, he permitted his desire to float upward like water rising in the rock pool, from his genitals to his lungs and to his head. All of this he felt was given to him on his own property. So he watched deliberately, for such was his privilege.

Just then he thought of Betsy, of Mrs. Emerson, in one of her characteristic positions: flower bed, weeding, pulling out roots and soil and hitting the root ends on the back of a shovel. For one moment the vision of Betsy, of Mrs. Emerson, and the younger woman stretched out beside the pool merged and blurred contrapuntally in his mind.

Below, the cabin door slammed.

The young man also walked from the cabin porch and down the stone steps. He was slender and young, his head watching his own feet carefully as he walked across hot shale. As Mr. Emerson watched, the younger man found his own ledge of stone, somewhat larger and immediately below the girl. Of this he was absolutely certain: the pair of them were on the same side of the pool, closer together than in the morning, or even at noon.

On their porch, in the dark, Mr. Emerson stopped rocking.

"On a cross-country hike, you said? Out here from Ohio to see some real country? Well, he came to the right place, it's all right here," and although his speech was benign, was totally conversational, he thought of what must surely happen when the pair of them went back up the steps and into the cabin to get something to eat: wouldn't they have to change clothes in the single room? Why, there was no privacy at all, in just the one single room.

"No harm in it," he added very easily for he understood Betsy was about to say, "What are you going to do about it, J.W.?"

Things between them went that way: in the first instance the cabin was her idea; therefore the rent money was hers to spend just any old way. Yet if something came up which had implications beyond the property lines of the ranch, something which might bring discredit on their home, then Betsy referred such matters to him.

"Why it's her privilege," Mr. Emerson said forthrightly, and saw no reason to interfere.

"Yes," and Mrs. Emerson saw J.W. was entirely right as she, herself, had said as much this morning. "She can have two-dozen guests—for all we care."

They went to bed.

Without consciously wanting to do so, Mrs. Emerson discouraged his hand on her thigh, much less on her breast. Having a new girl around the place would make a difference no doubt, and yet she said, "I weeded *all* day—and the side-bed does look better. . ."

Mr. Emerson heard the implication of her voice—and that was that.

Nevertheless, as was his privilege, Mr. Emerson recalled deliberately the sunlight on the vivid disorder of blond hair athwart an outcrop of shale. Then he caused himself to imagine the girl lying on the rock—like that—with no clothes on at all.

After one minute of abstract yet almost total satisfaction, without either guilt or remorse, he came back to his own responsibilities, and to what might be done if things got out of hand. "I'll get a look at her car registration. Sometime this week."

By then Mrs. Emerson was in the first shallow tide-pools of sleep, dreaming nothing at all.

IV

On the floor of the cabin, for more than ten nights, the boy slept on his blue, duck-down bag. When the sun came above the upper tier of redwoods each morning, he turned his face to the wall; in the large double bed across the room he heard Sands also change her position in order to avoid the light and in this way to sleep each day until ten o'clock.

Although it was his habit to rise early, the boy now took his daily patterns from Sands, and in this way he could think about everything: was there a larger pattern in that he had found this cabin only a few days after—by entirely different means—after Sands had also discovered it?

As to Sands, herself, it was still a puzzle. She seldom spoke, about anything. Mostly she worked by gestures of the head, of the hand. He wanted to know more, but he felt the last thing permitted him, as a guest, was to make direct inquiry.

So: if her name was Sands, was this after the novelist, or was it a family name? If she had left someplace very quickly, was she in flight from school, or family, or—perhaps—a boyfriend? Because she was so awkward in the kitchenette and could not make up a bed, had she ever worked, anywhere?

So: from her luggage tags and from a discarded envelope, she was connected with the Summer School at Arizona State University. Also about the Triumph automobile, Sands said ironically, "Why *his*. Wouldn't you *know* it?" Namely, her brother's car. She kept the car parked as much as possible. Why?

Beyond these few things, he understood Sands was thinking, allowing the sun to bake from mind and body the things she had abandoned, or fled, and which might still pursue her. Mostly because of an undefined pity, the boy made himself sensitive to her mood. Therefore he, also, used only a few words each day—and that was enough.

Finally, the boy felt he had earned the right to hold up the last, used and reused tea bag, and to laugh with her, and to say, "Sands, toss me the car keys?"

He drove back from Santa Cruz with many cardboard boxes.

Together, laughing a great deal because Sands really did like everything he brought back to the cabin, they stored the food on the shelves or in the refrigerator: one dozen assorted TV-dinners; packettes of Snax, Pretzels, Crackers, potato chips, E-Z Thins, and five water-tumbler deals of processed cheese, including a phoney Gorgonzola. Then Cola and Orange and Root Beer and two bottles of Cold Duck—all good stuff. In the last four boxes were the canned goods, the gut things to keep them eating well for quite a long time: smoked oysters, sardines, canned soups, canned crab and finally many packages of hot dogs, real buns, totally organic honey, and new-baked bread, 94 percent wheat germ. Finally he showed her the two top-twenty, long-play cassettes by the Leadfoot Family Four—*right* on.

After the initial food-run to Santa Cruz, the boy prepared all the food; he understood that unless someone took charge Sands only snacked and nibbled late at night while they listened again and again to the new cassettes. Cautiously he changed certain of their life patterns, but nevertheless each day they sunned on the rocks and talked about Mysticism and Faith; the Games Aspect of Life; and what happened, if anything, after so-called death. He was exactly three years younger, had gone to a private school, and had read a great deal; she seemed considerably older, said nothing at all about any high school, and tempered what he said by her "experience." By night, because it was softer, they now lay side by side on the double bed. When he turned off their light they listened, together, to the sounds of the night and the water filling the rock pool and to the water going away across boulders and down to the valley and to the sea beyond.

Several times they said it to each other: their relationship was very much like being brother and sister.

As the days passed they talked more and more about everything. Now they lay on the rocks with no clothes on at all because Sands wanted a perfect tan, with no strap marks showing. Finally they talked directly about sex, the thing he most wanted to discuss, but which until now, with every person he had ever known, had always eluded him.

"No," and the boy felt in all honesty she should know this final, unnatural, thwarted thing about him. "Not ever. With anyone."

Neither of them spoke. The sun overhead beat the surface of the pool like a drum.

In his own shameful confession he heard the real reason he had left home for the summer, and had elaborately disguised his intention as a "wilderness opportunity"; in fact, he had left home to seek something unknown and what he had found was a cabin among redwoods and a rock pool below.

In his voice she heard the irresolution, the shame, and the terrible lack of confidence in himself; all those things combined to form a desperate necessity for assertion not yet clearly understood even by himself. More than anything she wanted to say what he needed to hear, with no thought of the future.

"Oh, men mature much *later* than girls," she said and as she placed her hand on his arm for the first time she touched his flesh and felt a secret, tender satisfaction which always before had been kept from her. Then in order to experience this new feeling once more, she said, "Especially in a *boys* school. You just had no opportunity, you see?"

"Right," he said and he saw this was his exact case. Partly because he spoke to her outspread hair, he tried to be honest about it. "No opportunity—ah, that was *meaningful.*"

"But *you* have?" he asked directly for he wanted terribly to know this one very imortant, secret thing about her past. "*Haven't* you?"

"Oh all girls have to get around," and she said this not so much to his averted face as to the shelf of rock where they were sunning with no clothes on at all.

"That's what our English teacher pointed out about Milton: there is no such thing as cloistered virtue."

Those words meant nothing at all to her but everything instantly came back to her and it was as though the creek had suddenly risen, had overflowed its banks, had overwhelmed and washed away even the cabin.

From the very beginning she felt she had planned it so: the night of her fourteenth birthday party, with Ray, at his house, in his own room because. . . Then for a long time with Ken who was much more of a leader. Then the next year, in August, at the so-called Church Camp, it was a way to know everybody better, to be outstanding because. . . And then in high school, in Tucson, it was. . . and she braced her shoulders against the stone outcrop, as though all of the memories of the group in Tucson would go away.

By then even her own brother knew where she went every afternoon at three o'clock, and came home promptly at half-past five when her father always said, "Well, what did you learn today?"

Math, he always said, was very important.

The officers in plain clothes visited the high school. They searched lockers. They found what they though was a lot of stuff. Then it was "confidential" interviews which only the PTA, the Sheriff's office, and the high school newspaper editor knew about. Before Christmas her older sister, who always knew it all, came back from Bennington "to help." Even her father, who now thought some things were even more important than math, did not suggest she attend college. The idea was to "reach maturity," and never again see the old high school crowd ever again, except. . . So she spent more than a year at home, in her own room, and nothing happened all.

Later friends of her mother got her admitted to an "experimental" Summer Session in California: success there indicated real college in the Fall. And naturally the family psychiatrist very much agreed: get away from home; get away from Tucson. That was the first step. But a step towards what?

In fact it was a step towards cashing the Summer Session check for tuition and fees; a step towards the bus which finally took her to Newport Beach to see her brother—where the car was. Her brother was nice but this time he said if she ever took his sports car again, they were really through.

So she drove his car away at two o'clock in the morning, drove north, and before noon turned off the freeway to avoid the Highway Patrol, and finally when she was ready to scream because of the sun, she had seen the Cabin-for-Rent sign beside the Emerson's mailbox. Had her brother already reported his missing car to the police? For sure, her tuition check had cleared her father's bank account.

All these things she had kept to herself, for after the first ten days in this out-of-the-way, secret place she understood absolutely that everything was a matter of coming to terms, of acceptance of herself. Partly because David arrived, partly because they had talked about so many things, but mostly because she had understood it was only herself which she tore into pieces, she had made up her mind: in two more days she would call her brother in Newport Beach to tell him the exact date she would return his car and also exactly how many miles were now registered on the odometer.

David was talking to her.

"For you, Sands," and he wanted very much to hear her confirm it, "It was. Well, meaningful? Always?"

"Yes," she said and she felt it was the only lie in her whole life she would ever tell him.

Although her eyes were closed against all of the past and against the drum beats of the overhead sun, she felt his hand for the first time stroking her shattered, outspread hair.

In a moment, abruptly, the boy stood up.

He had felt the first breeze of late afternoon. Therefore to protect her he went back to the cabin to put something on and to bring back an orange drink and her robe.

From the porch of the cabin, farther up the hill among ferns, he saw Mr. Emerson again repairing their water pump.

Late that night after the cassettes played again and again, after he had turned off the light, when everything outside except the creek was silent, the girl stood in the moonlight beside the bed. She reached down and took the boy's hand. When he was standing beside her, in a fine, new way, she pressed her body close to his. For the first time she felt his lips on her flesh—first only on her neck. . .

That night the girl began to teach him everything that she knew, but only a little at a time. Like giving lessons. Yes, like giving useful, necessary lessons to someone not at all a stranger, and yet not precisely a younger brother, but above all to someone who was no threat, and who was hers, from the beginning, alone.

V

"I cannot and I will not," Mrs. Emerson stated to J.W. from her side of their bed. "Cannot condone what they are now doing in broad daylight; will not condone the wrong and the sinful which might well bring a plaintiff suit and resultant scandal county-wide. . ."

Over the years Mr. Emerson had learned to wait. Often Betsy went on like this. In the end, nearly always, she listened to reason.

"Also, to judge by their garbage can, if it isn't paper or tinfoil, then it isn't food—and all our nice fruit in season. . ." She rolled once beneath the sheets. The totally brittle nature of all those TV-dinners, the boy's furtive food-runs to Santa Cruz, the identical music playing again and again until all hours, the total modernity of it offended. Taken together their days and their nights seemed so wasteful, so improvident.

From his side of their bed, Mr. Emerson did not confide his opinion. Besides repairing the cabin water pump more than once, he now knew even better places which looked right down into the cabin. Also on no particular schedule he carried away their trash; also he delivered letters from the boy's parents in Ohio. Putting everything together, he saw only two young people—lucky ones—who would probably stay on until Labor Day and then the whole thing would end naturally enough. If the girl was somewhat older, he was well pleased to observe she was not now quite so withdrawn, so silent. When she ran up the steps to get more letters from Ohio, she always said, "Many happy returns," and laughed, and threw back her hair, and then ran away to find the young man who was off someplace looking for new paths. Once he delivered the mail right to the door, and she was just getting into her robe. What was happening was maybe good for everyone.

"Out," Mrs. Emerson said. "Out *she* goes."

"No real harm in it," he said very firmly, and of course it was true: he imagined himself reared above that young woman, doing what was necessary, and yet at the same time accepting the fact that it was only an older man's notion, and not at all possible for him—and it never had been, in all his life. Yet he wanted to prolong their stay, for the benefit of all concerned. "You already have her money."

Because he had added nothing to the case, Mrs. Emerson said

nothing at all.

Partly to cover his own tracks, and partly to delay any possible trouble ahead, Mr. Emerson added, "I got a look at the registration. I jotted it down. Probably her brother's car. From Newport Beach."

"That's good," Mrs. Emerson said in a forgiving, conciliatory way, and ended it for tonight. An address and a two-dollar telephone call, and possibly a referral to the young woman's mother—if she had one—those things were now possible. It was a strength to know a name was written down on the back of an envelope, a little bit like having money in the bank.

And yet resentment was what she felt. Mr. J.W. Emerson was just a little too interested, had repaired the cabin pump once too often. If not personally interested in the spectacle, why not save time for all concerned by delivering their mail *and* at the same time collect their garbage?

She thought of herself, on hands and knes, weeding a flower bed. She thought of J.W.—no shirt on at all—sunning on a rock, lying between the two of them, lying between that David and that maybe out-of-work airline stewardess old enough to know better.

Even though she knew these images were neither true nor remotely possible, Mrs. Emerson lay awake for a long time listening again and again to the cabin's music.

VI

Two days after the operator put through Mrs. Emerson's telephone call to Arizona, the girl's mother arrived: first by air from the Great Southwest; then by rented car from the San Jose airport, direct. Mrs. Emerson's telephone directions were accurate and it was no trouble at all to find the county road, and the mailbox, and the lane.

First the mother accepted the kind invitation of Mr. Emerson to step into the living room for a little chat. Without it being said in so many words, Mrs. Emerson understood there had been trouble before—and not suprisingly if what we read in the newspapers is even half-true. Apparently there had been "professional help" in the not-distant past; and surely this second daughter had grown up between three over-achievers. Not good. Behind that, there was the City of Tucson, itself. And behind that. . .

Mr. Emerson managed to disappear from the living room before

Mrs. Emerson took the girl's mother to the gate and pointed out the roof of the cabin and the rock pool below.

"Why, I'd know it anywhere!" the girl's mother said in an indignant, suppressed way. "Why, that's Herbert's T-4."

Because Mr. Emerson got to the cabin first, the boy and the girl were now already up and dressed.

The boy wore hiking boots. The bed roll and a canteen full of water were already strapped in place.

The rest of it was no business of hers, so Mrs. Emerson turned back from the gate and walked to the house to wash the coffee service.

Mr. Emerson, however, checked the gauge on the Petrolane tank, and that way looked down on the three of them: the boy, with the pack on his back; the girl, for the first time wearing red slacks; the mother. Together they stood on the cabin porch, talking very politely for almost five minutes.

Before the mother and the girl went inside the cabin together, the boy shook hands and then without turning to wave he went around the edge of the pool, and on down a path to the lower stand of redwoods. By nightfall he would be in Santa Cruz where he had wanted to go in the first place.

When there was no one left on the porch at all, Mr. Emerson stood motionless in the ferns for a long moment. Then he decided he might as well get at it: there was still enough time left of this morning to repair some fence.

VII

Later, in mid-October, at about two-thirty in the morning, Mr. Emerson awoke: he heard an automobile stop in the ranch yard—no lights. He heard the gate above the arroyo open. He heard the automobile coast forward over gravel. The gate closed.

Without having to get up or even put on his shoes or go out beneath an overcast, October sky to make certain, he knew the girl had returned. Wouldn't she have hidden a key, or have kept a key from the time she rented during the summer?

What he felt was a sudden excitement—and a terrible pity. Without willing it so, he remembered her blond hair scattered in the desperate sunshine, and her evenly tanned flesh—and no strap marks. For a moment, he thought she had come back because of himself. But no.

Nevertheless, in that memory of her, he recognized all of the wasted—yet productive—years of his life. For a few weeks she had revived in him the failed passion of all their married life. Oh, he watched all right, but mostly because he had grown up in a different era, when to look was the only thing most men were able to do. But no, it could never work out. What he wanted was for the girl to stay in the cabin—either alone or with somebody—for a very long time.

Until daylight, there was nothing for it except to lie awake, his back rigid against the stone ledge of their mattress. After breakfast, casually, he might walk down to the cabin to see if it was an automobile, after all.

Later he told the Sheriff. After that he told the Coroner's people. He told them exactly what he had seen and had thought. He started with the moment he first opened the gate:

Unbeknownst to either Betsy or himself, probably during the morning hours, this small Chevy sedan had parked beside their little rental place.

That seemed strange. Therefore he checked the locks on the cabin: no sign of entry, illegal or otherwise.

When he turned from the cabin door, why naturally he looked down the steps and into the rock pool. That's when he saw the body. Half-afloat it was and very steadily turning around and around with the current. Quick he ran down the steps because it had to be the same one who rented during the summer. It had to be the same one because even from above, on the steps, her blond hair floated in an odd, spread-out way.

If there were needle marks or any kind of puncture marks anyplace on the girl's body, the Coroner kept it out of the autopsy.

As for the boy, David, he was easy enough to check: he answered the telephone himself and had been all week in his dormitory at Oberlin College. The Sheriff did not disclose the nature of the case, but said only that this was a routine call.

"A terrible thing for the girl's parents," Mrs. Emerson later told the interested neighbors. "Both parents professional people, the mother with a Masters in Economics. Also a tragedy for Tucson, and to all those who knew her."

Privately, however, Mrs. Emerson surmised the girl came back to do what she had intended to do in the first place. But because the cabin was so nicely situated—with its view of the creek, and the valley beyond—and everything inside so nicely furnished, why no doubt that helped delay the girl's plan—for a time. And then Mrs. Emerson always added, "Of course, when she came back that second time, she was not really our tenant anymore."

When Mr. Emerson heard Betsy say that, he understood it was her way of making cetain the little rental cabin did not get a bad name.

Foss, A Cat Suburban

F or awhile I kept two people, but one had to go.

After I let Helen discover me in her garage the two of us lived alone right here at Mountbank Terrace. Then, as they say on afternoon TV, into our lives comes the gent N.K. (real name later). In a two-bedroom house, three's a crowd; so now it's only Helen and me forever. That's what I am telling you: how it's done, and my net results. This way you will learn something from Foss and—in all honesty—that's more than you would ever get from N.K.

At first you will say, "Oh how real tragic about Helen and N.K." Then you will see my side of it and you will say, "Well, Foss is a good one"—giving credit where due. As for myself, I say this: on the whole South Side and all along Mountbank Terrace to the freight yards everyone gets what they deserve—songbirds and veterinarians included. So judge for yourself.

So when you drive past our little two-bedroom house on Mountbank you will see Cordially Yours stretched out on the roof in the shade of the chimney doing my Bird Act—and waiting for Helen to return from Prudential to fix my dinner; you will see me up there all stretched out and tawny and you will say, "Good looking cat . . . watch out, birds." That is also exactly what Helen thinks when she thinks—which is not very often. If my life style is largely dramatic, my real interest has to be with net results.

But first, my gackground.

I'm practically all Persian, but no papers; furthermore, I'm practically all female (details later). I don't believe in Astrology, but maybe I really am a Gemini. Anyway, two days before Christmas with snow up to your tailfeathers a spoiled-rotten kid threw me out their automobile window at thirty-five miles per hour. I mean it: a spoiled-rotten laugh and out goes Foss at thirty-five per and hit clawing the driveway ice and skidded ass-over-appetite into Helen's garage door, *ker-zonk*. Naturally their automobile drove right on because the whole family was out driving around in the snow, at noon, to let the kids throw out the whole litter.

Maybe it really was a miracle: I meowed—like this—and up rolled Helen's automatic garage door. Saved: a well-lighted, wide-open, neat, dry garage. That's exactly where I was when Helen came home half-loaded from the Prudential Christmas office party: in plain sight on the garage work bench, curled up and plenty appealing in a blue ceramic bowl. That's how we met.

"Oh you cute little, poor little, sweet little, homeless kitty!"

At the time I did not know how our relationship might develop. I knew only the facts: outside it was dark, and getting colder; inside it was light and warm. So I purred it up very loud and Helen snuggled me against her imitation lambskin collar.

"Are you a boy or a girl kitty?" was what Helen said—as though *that* mattered. But, Doctor, nobody raises *my* tail. I mean it.

I yowled—and up again went Helen's garage door.

"*You* did it!" and Helen, who is a dummy about all machinery except a steno pad, held me tighter than ever.

Right then I understood a very important item. When Helen returned home her garage door was open. Because Helen lived alone, she was frightened of daylight burglars. When Helen believed cute kitty actually yowled open her garage door, she felt relieved: no boogey man inside. Naturally I was very young at the time, but I saw my angle: I gave Helen both a sense of security *and* someone to love. If true, at her age, weren't those two items alone worth some real considerations? Or look at it this way: the more for me, the better for Helen. That's still my policy.

Helen carried me into our house. I liked the color scheme: beige and light green and off-white; nice drapes; an imitation-brick fire-place. Now I understand our decor is fairly standard stuff; even then I felt Helen's black, ceramic leopard on the mantle was a little too much—Freud notwithstanding. Above all, I liked two items: our TV set and our really big picture window. Being disadvantaged, I cannot read, but I'm real visual-minded. In the past five years, on TV and through the window, I've seen plenty.

Finally, that first night, Helen sobered up and improvised an average litter for Cordially Yours in her spare bedroom, and then urned off the lights.

As I lay there in the dark, I realized the longer I put off my next move, the more difficult it would be for both of us. When Helen began to sleep off all that sauce from Prudential I "instinctively" gave her my Night Yowl #3.

If Helen wanted any more sleep, she had one choice. Therefore he moved my litter into our bedroom. When I curled up on her pillow Helen naturally heard my poor little heart go *beat-beat-beat* in the darkness. Finally Helen went to sleep but I lay awake for a long time trying to separate blind chance from the facts of what was unquestionably a very important day in my life. To go in a few short hours from a snowdrift to a warm, bedroom pillow was brute luck. As regards facts, I *knew* it was colder outside, and Christmas on the way. So I said "yes" to that fine, dry, gas heat of Helen's bedroom.

That's what I am telling you: how it all started, and my net results.

II

Comes now the gent N.K. (real name later). For awhile N.K. made a very great deal of difference at #27 Mountbank, but not anymore.

But before the N.K. wrap-up, so that you can note my total approach, I give you a typical day from my first two years with Helen. Up at 8 a.m., with Helen doing my breakfast. Then to the TV set for the morning weather and traffic reports, both items to me of only academic interest. After all, my weather inside was always correct and South Side traffic to the Prudential Building is not my territory.

Regards TV, it is worth mentioning how I arrange for Helen to leave it turned on all day for my educational purposes. You see, I understand very well that Helen really is frustrated, and is always more or less edgy. Therefore each morning exactly when she is slamming doors I make a pass at her nylons, or boost her purse off the dresser, or do my No-Claws Backscratch Act on a chair leg. Any item from that set *always* makes Helen scream. Depend on it.

"Naughty-kitty! Naughty-girl! . . . etc.," and in this way Helen works it off before office hours. Ninety percent of the days she neglects to switch off our TV.

That way I am tuned in for eight hours of news and information.

At six in the evening, when the garage door rolls up by itself, I hit the TV cut-off switch and when Helen walks in I am "asleep" in front of the refrigerator.

"Wakey time," Helen always calls out. Then she always says, "Eaty-time with Mommy Helen."

Oh, absolutely her diction makes me sick, but I also like fresh kidney every other day. Show Foss a kidney, and Foss will show a net result.

You say Helen is a silly woman, with a heart as big as a bird cage; I say Helen needs Cordially Yours simply to keep her on edge. Otherwise, all the Helens of the world might have to face life as it is. To face life without illusion is never easy, neither for Helen nor for the whole Prudential crowd—our gent N.K. included.

And I'm not a bum or a hippy freeloader. In fact, everyday I fulfill the real-life needs of Helen and also of her friends. Jot down these three versions of the same set: my Mole Act, my Mouse Act; my Bird-Pounce Act.

My Mole Act is useful when Helen entertains the other ladies from the offices at Prudential. They unload at the curb from two or three cars. They take off their colored glasses. They stare at our well-tended yard and say, "Wow, nice setup." Exactly when they cluster through the gate, walking in their summer dresses, I come out of the shrubbery. I am *very intense,* dragging my belly on the grass. Like this.

Suddenly I explode off the grass. I go past them purse-high and claws out. I hit beyond the walk. I claw up a furious cloud of dirt. They hear my "Mole Kill" yell. They see a mole come up, and out, and Foss on top. Then all they see is a streak of yellow tail, and that's me, going away, going low around the corner of the house. Many screams.

The Mouse Act presents less action: during cocktails I bring in a piece of skin or a tail and place it on their sandwich tray: solid revulsion for all concerned.

My Bird thing is suggested above: me lying in the shade on the roof, waiting for a sparrow or a big blue jay to land. It's a great feeling to float down like a shadow and make a cloud of bird feathers in front of the picture window. My fans scream plenty— but they are all behind glass.

My personal advantage, in the above?

First, I illustrate that Foss is cruel, destructive, *and* primitive;

herefore Foss cannot change his nature. When they admit that, I
have a license to go on this way forever. *Prima facie,* the Helens
at Prudential and the whole world *need* a great many "legitimate"
creams. If not from Cordially Yours, then who else can do the
job? N.K.? Don't make me laugh.

Deep down Helen likes to see cruelty, but being with Prudential,
she can't afford it. To her I'm real dangerous, but also safe. You
see I know one fundamental thing: at the psychic level, Helen never
really *does* anything. Furthermore, as illustrated below, her life is
all the better for it.

At this point my fans will ask two related questions: how does
Foss arrange "kills" in public? Second, why should Foss catch a
stupid mole when every Tuesday he is *given* a superior grade of raw
liver?

Not one fan in ten will see the correct answer: I do not hunt.
Ever.

Right: I have neighborhood contacts. Any day I can borrow a
dead mole; any time a half-dozen individuals are pleased to deliver
a dead mouse to Cordially Yours. Birds are different; birds never
learn. Every time they land on my grass to eat one of my "planted"
worms it costs them some tailfeathers. Actually, I do my Bird
Thing for the pure experience: for that long glide down from the
roof. Try it yourself sometime.

Comes now, N.K.

"Why, it's a *N*ice *K*itty!" so said the gent upon first arrival at
Mountbank Terrace. I'll never forget that day.

His real name was Eldon Haslett, Actuary at Prudential and so-
called systems-oriented manager. Because he was a guest, I gave
him a quick ankle-rub—and strictly no encouragement.

"Ve-ry friend-ly," and N.K. scooped me up.

"Female," says N.K., which shows one side of his mind.

Nobody, *nobody* raises *my* tail.

"She-it!" N.K. yelled, and in mid-air I ripped his other hand and
landed swinging above him on the chandelier.

Looking down between light bulbs, I saw Helen run in from the
kitchen.

"Is baby-kitty hurt?"

N.K. wrapped a handkerchief around his finger. While swinging on the chandelier, I saw that mean, secret, actuary look on N.K.'s lips. He asked for it: now he blamed me. From that moment on, as they say on TV, it was N.K. or Foss and no spread this side of the Pecos big enough for the two of us.

Helen coaxed me down. To demonstrate something elementary about territorial imperative, I snuggled tight against Helen's throat. Round One.

In two days, Mr. NiceKitty, NiceKitty was back. Then it was Beefeater time, and no TV for Cordially Yours. In two weeks drinks led to "dinner at home" and a pork chop bone past midnight for Cordially Yours. Then it was night rides in his Galaxy, with me in back, scared silly that N.K. would throw me out at fifty-five per—and no snow on the ground. Come Labor Day, and N.K. barbecued: Hell's own flames in the backyard, fat in the fire, and afterwards a long, slow walk around the block past dog yards—an exercise hitherto avoided. Things went from bad to worse.

That's why I was on the house roof for a long time in the sun of mid-October, trying to see things from Helen's point of view. I had to give N.K. all of the best of it: his paid-for Galaxy would gross out at $3,895; also he had above-average clothes in beige and blue and charcoal. Furthermore, N.K. claimed he hated dogs but maybe he just said that to please Helen. On fundamentals, I saw Eldon was steady, and a little dumb, and he was here, and I had to put up with it.

Just then a real nice young blue jay landed below me on the grass and began to play Drill Sergeant. I did not move a paw. That will show you the exact psychic state of Cordially Yours in mid-October.

That night N.K. went too far.

"Saaay," and he said after long silence—and his third Beefeater. "Our Foss is in heat."

"Ohhh?" Helen said, and put her head on N.K.'s shoulder. I was looking down from the mantle, one paw around the black ceramic leopard. When Helen snuggled a little closer, I saw what was on *her* mind. But—as alleged—N.K. was dense along certain lines.

Maybe both parties experienced that identical little feeling; maybe both parties were actually talking to each other, but outloud they were referring to me.

"Ought to . . ." N.K. said—and I nearly fell off the mantle—

"Have Foss fixed. Y'know?"

"I've *thought* about it," which was a lie because Helen never really thinks about anything.

"Unless," and N.K. went on softly. "Unless we keep Foss. Ah, for breeding purposes."

Right then, I jumped.

I gave Eldon the Mole Kill and the Bird Thing all in one. I went over his head, and hit running at the bottom of the drapes.

"Saw a mouse!" Helen yelled.

When I led N.K. around and around the room he turned over a chair. Then a floor lamp. Finally I took him through the garage, and outside into the rose bushes.

That's where N.K. lost me and also one nonexistent mouse. I hid under the garage-roof overhang, and watched for the Galaxy to head for home.

Even so I stayed there for a long time, to think. Beyond my own self-interest, I thought of Helen's welfare. So I made a policy: never, ever, did I want Helen to mate with anyone.

And of course Helen never did. See ending, below.

III

Nevertheless, things got worse on Mountbank Terrace.

But first, as promised, an intimate detail.

In late November, they scheduled a very serious proposition: a visit down-state, to Carbondale, to meet Helen's parents. In between comes the intimate detail of why to this day I'm practically all female.

Some of the facts are sordid. In private Helen began to stand naked in front of her mirror, making remarks to me about "losing her Summer tan." I saw two things: Helen really does have an oversized butt, and what she really wanted was a romp with N.K. in the shrubbery.

Maybe somewhere in my personality I have a coarse streak, but I will say this: if an individual is going under the shrubbery, then *do* it. Get some dirt on your belly, and take the consequences—if any.

That's my total philosophy of sex, but with Helen and Eldon-baby it was mostly Beefeaters and talk. Yet I sensed it: the *tone* of our house changed a little everyday. I avoided all thought about the different ways it could end—for me. After the fact, I realized they must have discussed it several times. After the fact, I very well can imagine exactly how their conversation went:

—You don't want our Foss to have kittens. *Do* you?

—Oh, no.

—But we want to keep our Foss for a pet. Don't we?

—Oh, yes.

—So while we are in Carbondale, I'll just have the job done. I have a friend.

—Oh?

—Sure. And this job's on me . . .

Helen was and is a little money saver. So no doubt the money was one consideration. If you worked for Prudential, could you be otherwise? No matter, the deal was made.

"Nice Kitty Nice Kitty," was the way N.K. woke me up on that fateful afternoon just two days before Christmas. I was asleep on Helen's side of the bed, under the covers.

N.K. did his own Mole Act: he *pounced.*

"Gottcha," and it was a quick scruff-grab and there I was in an onion sack, and headed West on Hyster Avenue in N.K.'s Galaxy.

I skip the sordid details. I merely confirm that the two-story stucco building on Hyster is a very antiseptic, very high-pressure, very nice, and a very sinister veterinarian's hospital.

"Here's the victim," N.K. said very cheerfully, and threw onion sack and all on the reception desk.

"Per our arrangement. Bill me." N.K. said, and walked out the door and into the snow whistling "Deck the Halls . . ."

Some hours later I woke up with a head as big as a dog bone and all the attendants home for a long weekend. Water, there was none. I slept.

Sidelight: at the desk the Vet's wife quoted N.K. a private recuperation cage, but the young Vet reneged, and the house kept the difference. That way N.K., the Discount Kid, got taken. And he had a lot more coming. From me. Personally.

Nevertheless, while the young lovers (ha-ha) risked their lives on the highway going South to Carbondale, I reviewed the facts. No post-op complications, and that was good. I still had my good looks and all that Persian know-how. And being *practically* all female might have advantages—not that I would go out as a matter of policy looking for shrubbery-action.

I concluded two things. If both parties of interest had used me only to act out their own frustrations, then nothing, between them, was basically changed. Secondly, on that fateful afternoon, in fact, had not N.K. bought an interest in my future? Wouldn't he now have to protect his investment? I wanted to believe so, but I could not be sure. Even if Eldon had a good job with Prudential, you could not always depend on his logic.

IV

"Clumsy life at its work and ha-ha" was what I said in February when Prudential management very wisely sent N.K. on the road for two months. In my territory the gents who only telephone from say Huntsville, Alabama, always finish last. On percentage I felt good: N.K. was out of town, and maybe out of our lives forever.

Naturally I was not amused that night in Spring, just after the final weather and news, when the Boy Actuary checked in. Absolutely unannounced he rang the doorbell. With arms outstretched, Eldon yelled, "Hey!" and only after the clinch did I see he had come back with a very great deal up-front. He had a new "Skylark" at the curb, a basket-weave, Italian silk suit, and in-hand a box of semisweet chocolates, that last item, incidentally, not recommended either by the Good-Doctor Foss or by Helen's bathroom scales.

In less than two days, everything went bad. At once all parties of interest revived the Beefeater Tradition—first on the couch and then on the rug. Again it was Cordially Yours on the mantle, and plenty of rough stuff above and below the belt—but no decision. In my opinion N.K. was not remotely a natural-born handler. Prejudice aside, over on Rackney Boulevard I know a Black Tom who takes on a lot more territory—and no complaints.

What I always thought possible, finally happened.

Helen took over.

Finally she had to say it: "Eldon," she said, "I love you." She said it just like that. Sort of flat.

". . .Ohhh, Eldon, I do. I dooo . . ." which was more like it.

"I . . . I got to . . ." and Eldon was still trying to add up the column.

"We are right. For each other," and Helen kicked up one bare foot from the rug.

"Ba-by . . ." and N.K. used his Nice-Kitty voice.

Being somewhat excited, Helen did not catch his tone. So she made the mistake she should have made at least one year previous. She got up off the floor and took N.K.'s hand and led him to our bedroom.

Maybe I can't read, but I sure can listen. And don't give me that "prurient interest" stuff. Absolute *self*-interest put me up on my hind legs outside the door: getting a hot-line on the action.

Being where she was at the moment, I had to laugh when Helen said very distinctly, "Oh Eldon. We shouldn't . . ."

Right then I did what I had planned to do from the second day N.K. ever showed up in that cheap Galaxy.

I waited three full minutes. Then I kicked the black ceramic leopard off the mantle. Down she fell—and exploded on the bricks.

Helen came out.

"Hurt! Kitty's hurt!"

N.K. followed Helen and it was something to see: both parties wearing nothing at all except last Summer's tan.

N.K. kicked once, and then tried to scuff-grab me.

That's when I put eight good claws on his shoulder, and vaulted up and over to the chandelier.

"Som-bitch. I'll gittcha . . ."

So I swung twice and hit the drapes in a get-away slide. Then right back into the bedroom. I was stretched out full length on the carpet directly under the bed.

"So scared," Helen said very softly, and changed the subject.

I winced a little. "I duuu Louuuve Youuuuuu . . ."

I made my move.

What N.K. heard first were my claws. He looked up and there, hanging loose on the headboard, looking down with eyes as bright and as big as fish bowls, was Cordially Yours.

I opened my mouth—like this: showed him my big white, back teeth.

"Cat! Cat!" and N.K. took one long, mean swipe at the headboard. And missed.

He fell on Helen, but he swung again.

That time he hit the carved, mahogany bedpost that in the moonlight looked like a big, curled-up Tom.

"Som-bitch!" and N.K. rolled out to finish me.

A long diagonal of moonlight coming down through the drapes lighted my target area.

N.K. never did see me coming in: it was my Bird Thing, claws out and ass high. I landed right on his Robin.

N.K. let out a Mole-Kill Scream Number Four. While he found has pants, I made it out through the kitchen and to the garage-roof overhang.

That's where I was when all house lights came on. That's where I was when Helen said, "Shit," and where I was when N.K. called her something worse, and I was still there, and shaking a little, when the first door slammed.

A prettier sight you never saw than the red taillights of his Skylark disappearing for the last time down Mountbank Terrace.

In a few minutes Helen came to the back door in her blue night-robe. She called out into the night, calling for the one thing in life on which she really could depend. Having the advantage, however, I naturally took my own slow, sweet time checking in.

That night Helen cried and cried and finally went off to sleep. The very next day, however, everything was pretty much back to normal: I mean for me, and for her, and for the whole South Side. By October Helen was again leaving the TV on all day, and once again it was a superior grade of liver for Cordially Yours.

So much for how it all came out, and my net results. I do, however, want to add a few additional remarks for the record.

First, I want everyone to know that on fundamentals Helen is more content and more happy than ever before. She never mentions the other Nice-Kitty gents at Prudential. I call that genuine renunciation: it can only lead to more spiritual growth for all concerned. If Helen was really unhappy, I would be the first to know. Besides, feelings are secondary; only actions signify.

So, in fact, what does Helen do all day long?

Mostly I can tell you about our nights. For example, at my meal-time, I insist that Helen eat some of my food, just to try it, just so she will better appreciate my point-of-view. She likes that. It's so humanizing.

Then when our lights are turned off, I teach Helen to play like a cat. She gets behind the chairs, and behind the sofa. Now she can curl up on our coffee table.

Next month we will get down to fundamentals. Maybe it is only role-playing, but Helen has got to learn to run like a mouse. Then I'll chase her—just for the experience.

Helen really wants to try that, and for Helen it will be easy. We will work on it every night, right up until Christmas.

Why don't you try it yourself sometime, with your own pet? For the experience.

The Other Kingdom

I did not at once gain their confidence.

Now, however, I live in a house beside marshlands that stretch rustling towards the shut-down Potash Works, and all night I listen very intently but hear only the jet aircraft in the overcast, burning towards the runways. Beneath these sills I know storm sewers converge, then lead offshore to the first shelf of the sea. Not there, but by parallel to your own city lies their Other Kingdom.

Twice I talked calmly with your government (city) officials—told everything. Twice behind my back they winked slyly and said, Is that so? Whereupon I moved secretly to this house. But isn't it now only a matter of time?

Obsession is no issue. What began in innocence became disinterested study; from understanding came the final intimacy of full knowledge—as they had planned from the beginning. (Fully explained, below.)

Even as a boy my instincts were normal (in all respects). That spring an Ohio thunderstorm had just passed across the town. At noon by the pond's edge, between a railroad siding and the maze of cattle pens, my terrier foraged the cattail stalks. Suddenly, overhead, the sky was a split-open bale of sunshine; my airgun barrel became a straight tube of purple light. Beneath the great steel tick-tick of noon, I saw a round, grey stone twitch—then run. As though a woman's stocking nylon floated up the post, and then trotted in full view across the top board of the cattle pen, shining, outstretched against the clouds and the red water tank beyond, I saw it.

My terrier rose upward from the gravel, seemed for a full minute to remain suspended in mid-air until he struck flat against the cattle pens yelping. The dog fell back. But the rat (*Rattus Norvegicus*) was gone.

Hatred was what I felt. From that moment until I was eighteen and moved to your city, I killed them. I harried them from Kennet's barn; by cage-trap and immersion in water, alone, I cleansed the Slaughter House. Where their incisors chewed the upholstery of cars in wrecking yards, or where they ran on beams across the grain elevators, I pursued them. Or so The Old allowed me to believe, at the time.

All *highly approved.* (Note: very central to character.)

In the home, highly approved by my grandmother, for I lived with her after my father was killed in the woods. In the schools, highly approved by all teachers who knew from my oral reports and my display boards about the row-upon-row of tails, labeled and dated very nicely; likewise from my early paper in Social Living, "The Rodent: Familiar Haunts." I still retain my government pamphlets: "Breeding for Profits"; "The Threat of"; "Safe and Sane Poisons"; "Controls: Warehouse and Dock." (See tin-lined boxes, East basement wall.)

From the first my "interest" was noted. The first little story appeared in our high school news. Staring back at me from an inside page, I saw a young boy: ears perhaps overly large, the two nippy black eyes close together, the nose and chin coming to a distinct, intelligent point, and my smile—so engaging then—highlighted by my two large upper front teeth (not overly large). Boyish, outgoing. I was the very picture—of myself.

And who could have known my apprentice years were also their Phase I? After all, had not The Old ones already engaged my interest?

One day with my government pamphlets and anatomical drawings packed neatly in suitcases, I came to your city. Slender of hand, clever at traps, mother not heard from since they found my father dead in the woods, I first saw the buildings of your city. There I heard what I knew was the *real* world humming in the washed-white dawn of youth. Alone I came there not to seek my fortune, but to pursue disinterested knowledge for its own sake.

Those first weeks perhaps you saw me walking the streets, looking intently at bouquets of flowers behind plate-glass windows. Later I rented clean airy rooms not far from a midtown university. Because I was a specialist, they hired me; daily I walked between cages wearing my white smock. There I witnessed experiments in psychobiology concerning drugs and memory. But at night, in my rooms, I studied much alone.

After heavy rains I heard water running in the storm sewers beneath my bed. Late one night, past Christmas, I discovered—and then articulated—the first sullen phonemes of their language. By way of sounds uttered in my own throat began the bridge, the long way to knowledge, the way into their Other Kingdom.

In personal habits I remained chaste (in all respects).

II

No matter. After hours, in my rooms, I had trained twelve *Rattus Albans* to trip the latch of their cage at sunrise and to pull the cord on my Venetian blinds. I can now believe this activity, done in unison, served as an ur-language: their movements in concert was something like music and was therefore understood by The Old without transliteration. (Complete explanation below.)

Therefore imagine my joy when I heard the first voice: that voice was intelligence, oh sought-for communication:

-Beet—Veat?

Their first envoy, at noon, was in the center of my study, in a diagonal ray of sunlight. She sat on haunches, light fawn in color, her exceptionally broad, wide-eyed face looking upward into my face.

Unquestionably, I say "she" because of the feminine timbre of the voice. As beside the cattle pens, in the burst of sunshine, I sat transfixed. Then discipline took over.

"Meat-meat?" I said in a high-pitched tone. I was on my knees, but not too close.

From my kitchen I brought back two squares of roast beef.

-Beet—Veat! she said, and in two trips returned the squares of beef to the refrigerator. I heard the refrigerator door swing open—and then smartly close. At once I knew: here was a higher order of kinetic capability.

Precisely then, I understood: their Other Kingdom is a version of our own, and therefore is roughly parallel in both patterns of conduct *and* in language. Therefore their "v" is our sound "kn."

-Kneef—Kneef!

I handed over my small pearl-handled pocket knife, the one I had carried since boyhood. I held the knife, unopened, in the sunlight. I placed it gently in her overly long, highly articulate "fingers."

Without haste, but with great excitement, the most wonderful one I had ever seen turned, and still upright, vanished as though by liquifaction into the shadow of my bedroom closet.

Date: 26 February.

At sunrise the next day the twelve I had trained with such great labor ran in unison across my bed and very mechanically closed the blinds. For the first time I saw those twelve were of a lower order, perhaps genetically inadequate. By noon I had destroyed them. With their destruction I had left behind an epoch. I had stepped from an encircling woods into the first meadow of their Other Kingdom.

-Ieets—Ieets?

Two more of the fawn-colored order—save one shade darker— came back at noon. Upright they stood, in the sunshine of winter. In unison their voices spoke. Their articulate "hands" were outstretched in supplication.

At once I understood their new request.

"Steel, steel?" and I gave them two old razor blades from my bathroom cabinet. My usual scientific detachment, as when I walked between cages wearing a white smock, suddenly gave way to mere speculation. Passionately, I wanted them to converse. Could they really operate simple machines? (See below, "At the Forge.")

Yet how unaware I was about the larger issue of their plan. Even then I could actually believe they needed only metal with a cutting edge: *Ieets,* or *Fnor.* (See, "Their Metallurgy: Contamination, Toleration, and Release." Journal #6.)

III

Notes: all their data is held in "files"; this information is passed on by rote. Each individual memorizer (Slave, Class 5) is the equivalent of one manila file folder; each memory-group aligns tribally (i.e., by the subject matter they remember). To eliminate a body of knowledge, The Old denies those files (individuals) food. The Old, however, are also "files" of past *Ianimret* decisions; they, therefore, combine both jurisprudence and causistry. (See my tin-lined boxes, clothes closet.)

[Noted ascendencies: much like our own organized crime syndicates, each "state" of their Other Kingdom has traditional boundaries. Their government (equivalent to our exploitation) is dictated by The Old. Their supreme *Ianimret* (our Senate) convenes in their Capitol. Politically Fascist, all edicts are enforced by the *Sub-Ianimret* wardens, as follows: Public Works (i.e., our destruction); Welfare (our Prisons Bureau); *Iaerec* (Foods); Health (our hatcheries, pig farms, and other breeding establishments). Planned feeding aligned with forced breeding fills all worker requisitions. Their State itself is conceived by them as an *Iaerec-Inc* food-getter) system. Our central concern is "salvation"; their obsession is to obtain total food-world.]

Query: being authoritarian, does this account for the total absence in their language of our signals for "thank you"?

Those things I did not at all comprehend until I followed down into the storm sewers beneath my bed. Gradually, those sewers became illuminous because of phosphorescent algaes. Suddenly the passageway became incredibly small. Only by kicking and squirming did I pass into a larger room, and then, by tunnels, into the chambers of The Old.

In the presence of The Old, in a halting version of their speech, I made a formal statement. I declared Good Will. I announced a good new Era of Communication. I declared—symbolically—an end to all prejudice between their domain and our world.

In unison I heard The Old reply, using my exact intonation, my precise words. Significantly, however, they repeated the last phrase: they declared an end to all prejudice—and all causes thereof.

That we could both understand this problem—and could agree—seemed to give my life a new meaning.

The three members of The Old were exceedingly broad-faced, intelligent. I had a dual impression: their polish was that of successful executives the world over; secondly, there seemed to be a illuminosity about their presence which I felt very strongly. There were no other preliminaries.

-Loitamrofni, Loitamrofni! In tone their shouted order was absolutely military.

In the mouth of a nearby tunnel a "file" appeared. Before entering our conference chamber the "file" hesitated. Being administratively trained, he awaited further orders.

An *Araug* (guard) snatched the informant and threw him with great force at the base of their three-sided desk.

Still dazed, the "file" very mechanically began to speak.

Behind the desk, on their scoop-like chairs where they half reclined, The Old attentively watched the expression on my face.

I heard a shrill outflow of names, places, dates. This file concerned a project of long standing, and of great importance to The Old. What I heard was a thousand details of my own life: from the cattle pens, to the first words we exchanged: *kneef-kneef.* It was their version of my life, seen from "below." Having repeated the contents of its mind, the "file" turned his back on the three-sided desk.

Possibly a signal was given. More probably custom prevailed. But the information having been conveyed, the individual (a fawn-colored male) was struck down from behind with a truncheon.

The Old were already standing. Without another sign they led me through an exceedingly dry tunnel, downwards, towards the flames.

From a balcony I looked out across a low, vaulted industrial room. The flames burned in a row of separate forges. As their smithies worked metal, the sparks flew upward towards my eyes.

Beside the sixth forge we stopped. A thousand small sticks seemed to snap, but this noise was their hammers of stone tap-tapping in the wind-sound of the bellows. Above each forge, running in harnessed teams of six inside a wheel, the largest ones I had ever seen made the bellows pully spin.

The forge-worker ritualistically exposed his neck to The Old. When they did not strike him with a truncheon, the smith returned to his work.

Overhead the team running furiously inside the bellows wheel made the flames turn a fragment of blue steel to white heat.

-Your old razor blade, Sir.

Beside the forge, a cage door opened. A half-grown male came out. Its head was placed in a wedge of stone; the forge-master's assistants twisted the head in such a manner that: 1) the body was immobilized; 2) the white incisors were exposed to the smith's hammer of stone.

I witnessed twelve attempts. First the smith clipped off an "ingot" of razor-blade steel. He held this metal first to his own nostrils. In panic he threw certain ingots at once into a pile of scrap. If he were satisfied *with the odor,* the smith then placed the white-hot steel on the worker's exposed teeth. If the subject screamed, he was struck with an iron bar and the body thrown with great force into a chute which led to the feeder pens below. If the specimen's body could accept the metal (i.e., if there were no visible spasm) the smith reheated the tempered steel.

Cleverly, the smith fashioned two cusps of steel. These caps were shaped to a cutting edge, then shrunk on the end of the exposed teeth. Thus shod, the blue razor-steel shining, the specimen was released. Joyfully he trotted past the other forges, splintering any pieces of wood in his way.

"Only one," The Old who was this day's spokesman said. "Only one worker's tooth in eighty can accept metal. This is our national tragedy."

And so it was: their bodies tolerated or rejected metals in direct proportion to individual intelligence. Being of a higher order, the smith first tried the hot metal on himself; only then did he give each worker a crude "Metal-Tolerance" test. Much later I understood why The Old wanted their second envoy to take a razor blade from my own hand. Nevertheless, I asked the obvious question, but The Old stared at me in disbelief.

"Force? We should use force?" The Old finally replied. "You suggest we forcefully cap *all* Class Five and Six and also our Out-Runners . . . ah . . ."

He explained that when force was used the worker first attacked the forge masters, and then used the steel-cutter teeth for the destruction of Self.

"Ahhh, but *if* we could!" and they threw back their heads and laughed and laughed. When they did a little dance step before the hot mouth of the forge I saw their own back teeth were capped with tips of gold.

"Then, Sir, would it matter if there were tanks of steel around your vegetable oils? or even dikes that keep back the sea?"

Because I wanted to help them, I suggested caps of nonferrous materials, perhaps diamond dust. Diamonds might be obtained at night from certain store windows .

Scornfully, The Old looked at me—savage that I was. The spokesman put it clearly:

"The wealth of nations is food-supply, *Iaerec-Vlppus.* This supply is in direct proportion to capability in steel. High-grade, tempered *Ieets,* Sir ."

Suddenly he paced back and forth along the row of forges. The teams running inside the wheels overhead stopped. He shouted at me:

"No more so than *you*, are we to be forever the have-nots, the citizens of the sixth class, denied the efficiency, the total food-getter capability of *every other race.* Our struggle is Just. Our dedication shall prevail! We shall overcome the national tragedy of *our own blood*, our unjust inability to accept, yes, to accept genetically what is there—" He pointed to the world above the ceiling of that room—"up *there* for our foragers, for the packing away by the ton, yes, and also it lies as ore on the very surface of the earth itself. Oh, give us *Ieets, Ieets!*"

The forge masters and the assistants raised their clenched fists. They also pointed upward towards their poured-concrete ceiling. The applause re-echoed and their voices began to chant:

-Steel-for-all; All-for-Steel. (*Ieets pof Ill; Ill pof Ieets!*)

Such was one side of their national character.

Later I viewed their extraordinary Maze Hall where the young—up from the farrowing pens—were directed to the specific warrens of the social structure. As we walked, everywhere, continuously, I heard feet running on stone, and pelts rubbing, rubbing through passageways; everywhere, continuously, I heard the dark thud of truncheons on flesh for in that place neither hope nor prejudice obtain. In their tunnels a fetid bran-smell hung like blue smoke even in their incubator stalls where crowns of females lay, their tails knotted, giving birth until they, themselves, were thrown down into the feeder bins, to be consumed by their own litters. We came then to the private chambers of The Old.

Daintily, The Old ate with their hands. To observe custom, I did the same. Our bran was warm, and tasted something like the fetid smell of the blue air.

"Therefore," I finally asked for they answered all questions very candidly, "was my father's death in the woods entirely accidental?"

"Not accidental. Our interest, however, was in his almost precise resemblance to us, The Old."

Intently, they looked into my face.

True, my father's shoulders had sloped forward when he walked; his small black eyes were close to a nose which was really overly long. Clearly, The Old had once believed my father's mere physical resemblance was enough.

"But not slain by us," The Old said. "Your mother ran away in a black automobile with the man who shot your father. That 'accident' was during squirrel season. His death naturally ended our interest—in his case.''

"So you turned to me?'' and everything that had ever happened in my life seemed to fall into place.

"But communication,'' said The Old, "is not . . .''

"Enough?''

"Precisely,'' and as we got up again The Old threw their wooden bowls with great force at the *Araugs*.

As we walked up ramps towards the light, The Old answered a final question concerning the tolerance of metal. Their Slave Classes are neither intelligent enough to select useful metals, nor are they genetically adequate to mouth-contacts with cutting or tempered steels. Therefore all metals must be *Aerutaned* (neutralized); this process is apparently an enzyme-triggered syndrome, systemic in nature. My pocket knife and razor blades explain all of this by example: as I affectionately trained the twelve *Rattus Albans* to pull my blind cord at a given signal, I also neutralized, in part, all objects of tempered steel within the radius of my bodily odors. That neutralization, however, was only mechanical in nature. Hence, communication—as they said—was not enough, was not totally efficient.

We stopped beside a heart-shaped door.

To my surprise, The Old handed me an all-white truncheon—probably a femur bone. The truncheon fit solidly into my hand.

When they stood aside, I entered the room alone.

This room was a bower, the walls of grey velvet, the floor ankle-deep in the skins from small, white animals. The dais was covered with pillows; I sat there for a long time, overwhelmed by the perfume of the moment.

An *Araug* appeared through a curtain of beads. After a ritualistic pause, a female entered.

She was tall, the face broad, the single white polished ornament—a tooth with a large polished cap of steel—fixed as a spot of light, a miniature crown, in the center of her head. I felt a terrible excitement.

At first she seemed to be no fixed color for she was of light, changing as she moved: first fawn, then doe-brown, and when in shadows the color of wet pearls.

Having curtseyed, she reclined on the dais. With pillows everywhere around her body, she looked up at me, eyes luminous and blue against the piled-high white skins of animals.

Desire, was what I felt. I, who was chaste (in all respects).

Ritualistically, the *Araug* kneeled before me—neck exposed.

My truncheon of bone seemed to rise by itself. With primitive force, I struck. Being now depraved by that act, I rolled the guard's body into the outside corridor. I did this in order to be here. Alone. Now.

For the second time I looked down into that face. The small skins of animals around the thighs quivered. The warm tip of the nose delicately touched the place where my shirt opened and exposed my own flesh.

And then she was mine (in all respects).

Afterwards, when as in a dream I saw the cereal factories of the world and the ground beneath skyscrapers give way beneath their tooth-armed assault, only then did I see the consequence of my act. What new tolerators of all metals might now be unleashed to bring the odor of bran and the dark thud of truncheons on flesh to all your cities? By my act I was now both their liberator and the new Adam of some dark teeming race.

Therefore, *only to save others,* I caressed that illuminous face with one hand. With my other hand I found the all-white truncheon.

I hesitated. In a moment of revelation in her eyes, I saw not only the calculation of all governments, but also a genuine loathing—her loathing of me.

I struck again, and yet again, outraging her flesh with my truncheoñ of bone.

Once back in the chambers of The Old, I feigned raptures. I also ordered that the bower be not disturbed for sixteen hours—to insure gestation.

In feigned anger—and for revenge—I called for the "file" of their knowledge about the slayer of my father, so long ago inside a smoky woods.

Carefully, I listened. I heard repeated many of your own names. I slew my informant. I threw the body with great force into the corridor.

Greedily, I pretended to bargain with The Old for all diamonds in all the windows of all your jewelry stores—when Their Day came. With appropriate military dispatch, I accepted their offer of Liaison Chief for the world—when Their Day came.

Very clearly at that moment The Old foresaw the days of wrath to come when a new race of *Araugs,* and every worker at the forge would come forth with steel-shod incisors glittering beneath the moon; would come like water running upward from storm sewers, then go beneath street lights and along freeways until they overflowed the lawns of paid-for houses, their teeth making the shrubbery scream, splintering at last the sills of the world. The eyes of The Old glittered. They cried out for joy.

At once I returned to my rooms near the University, carrying only the all-white truncheon.

Past midnight I fled (not on foot) past your city's edge and at last hid in this house beside a marsh that stretches rustling towards the shut-down Potash Works. But isn't it only a matter of time?

Until then, watch carefully for me in your city streets, especially at noon when I walk through crowds of Christmas shoppers, all prejudice forgotten—for the moment. At once you will recognize my overcoat of grey, the face which has eyes too closely spaced, the nose, admittedly a trifle long, the shoulders sloping unnaturally forward as I go. It is the grey face which always floats past, the one almost too eager to smile, to speak, to tell everything: the face, in fact, of all your love.

Nor will you smile slyly and say, Is that so? when we pass beneath the tinsel and the decorations in the chime-noises of noon. You dare not smile for certain of your own faces each week tell me this: you also have known that Other Kingdoms are haunted by a great longing to return. For in that place all men are born.

A Rumor of Metal

After nineteen years in this frightful climate, I remained extraordinarily healthy. Moreover I understood our Territorial Police mission in the midcontinent river basins. As I rose in rank from Constable to OC/OMT, I ran things by the Manual (as revised). Mine is a large territory; I know each creek. I shave every day and do not like people who make their own little rules.

No matter: towards the end of the Winter rains I was reviewing my Ops Reports of past years. Our Secure-Base people on the Gulf know only what someone—anyone—dispatches by down-river courier. My replacement was due any week and therefore I was reviewing *all* files—a conscientious thing to do.

At the time of that up-river incident—what, ten years ago?—the two boys were about nine years of age—and one had red hair. Even over the intervening years, vividly, I remember the red hair.

In re-reading my Ops report, I saw no harm in it—and nothing could ever be proved. Oh, possibly at the time my relationship with that Town-Major was a little bit special—nothing more . . . At two o'clock in the morning I was alone. Rain coiled and struck the wall and then ran like a many-legged animal across the shutter.

With that file in hand, I recalled everything—and especially the boy with the red hair. To be entirely candid, the moment of recall was also poignant: having been in the Old Mississippi Territory for so many years, and as yet not officially detailed to a Secure-Base on the Gulf, I was a father to no one. I felt very much alone, even bereft for in my hand I held the future of two boys.

That morning a renegade american came down-river to sell news. Astride his log, he had paddled two nights. Towards dawn he had rolled his log on to the mudflat below my Headquarter's landing. In the lee of his paddle-log, the american slept on the mud until the sun rose higher in the sky. Eventually he got up, scratched himself, and walked the slope towards my Headquarters: a verified cooperator, from a bluffs settlement, more than a day's go up-river on a tertiary stream.

I always keep informants waiting: it helps them organize their story.

Then for an hour I worked the american. My verified's execrable, broken speech was frontier hyperbole and lies. Nothing any of them *ever* says is either direct or descriptive; after so many generations their argot of defeat became the accepted language of a continent.

The more I listened to the verified, the more I understood he was reporting—possibly—some real metal. Moreover, he claimed this metal was "fabricated." But was his *story* fabricated? Or was this alleged metal "fabricated"? They always say "fabricated": It is their national obsession . . . *Osthot?*

In reply, the verified said one of two things: either this find was as big as a mountain; or, this big metal was inside a mountain. Something like that.

Rumor or fact, I was going up-river. If metal were reported, I would take immediate, appropriate action—and possibly pick up an extra levy of work-age males. I *know* they are not able to use metal, but field officers up-river also understand they secretly continue to "experiment," as though by merely "natural" procedures they might again fabricate something. Just suppose, against all odds, a non-verified found a process to use metal: wouldn't that be an actionable development? Wouldn't that thing spread, like some fatal, clandestine disease?

That's why a metal find, a cache, or even the rumor of metal is one thing never ignored in my Territory.

I called for my flat-bottom, the twelve-oar skiff.

My work is essentially river work. To follow even the rumor of metal I will go to the farthest reach of any tributary until my coaster-boat or skiff grounds on mud in one inch of water. Very much I value the oarsmen.

I was already dressed for patrol, was waiting at daybreak on the landing when I saw my best crew emerge from their barrack/boathouse. Six men on each side, they moved their legs in unison: a machine, a twelve-legged, running animal carrying my skiff. They launched, then leaped to their stations, almost as one person. Across each crew-member's back was a Go-bag: with their Go-bags of food they often live for one week aboard a skiff and through the daylight hours row steadily.

This particular crew pleased me. Any crew-chief, naturally, is a verified; this one was a small Black man, with a resonant, rowing, coxswain voice. Many a day in rain or nearly adrift, partly lost in the green fogs, we had worked the river and the creeks. He drove the oarsmen; I called the course and speed. He did his work; I did mine. We use americans to row.

Then it was noon on the sunlit water, the coxswain driving the oarsmen, their backs two lines of sweat-covered, precision sculpture in motion. Each year after the rains the channels are utterly changed. There is no vegetation for miles beyond the serrated river banks, but in Spring always I see a washed, dynamic beauty in the knobs of clay which stretch inland towards a mirage of blue, motionless smoke. This horizon-line marks the escarpments where shrubs first put down roots in granite. The day was cloudless, and the Black Coxswain's chanting voice at times seemed to echo down upon us from the sky.

To observe more closely another kind of change, I pointed my skiff through a break in what once was a levee of the east bank. Here the water sprawls inland across many square miles of barely navigable sloughs. These sloughs once were fertile valleys where rivers joined and flowed south to the gulf. And here, also, lay their cities: sunk like outmoded, ill-designed vessels of war, long ago covered by silt.

During the last rains, by chance, this channel had become almost straight; the skiff moved easily on ten feet of clear water across what once had been the edge of a town—a small one, a place now nameless, with not even a Survey Number on our charts.

Beneath the skiff's bottom the water unexpectedly became more shallow. To find deeper water, the Coxswain steered abruptly left between two clay humps. Ahead and below, lay the "main-street" of this town, its "roofs" a few feet beneath our boat.

The oarsmen pulled twice, then shipped the oars. We drifted without a sound, as though we were strolling, in springtime, along the sidewalks of another age . . .

Never had I seen the facade of a town so precisely outlined: the current had swept the gutters clean; in store fronts the display windows still faced the street. One window display, anchored in light silt, was nearly complete: a child's three-wheeled, wooden toy, with the carved head of a horse; a square, picket-sided crib for a baby; terra-cotta heads of dolls, all in a row, their eyes now vacant holes; yes, and three wooden, toy guns, still pointed at the running water of the street. In two weeks, on the surface, the summer algae would grow again. This street, accidentally exposed, would be cut off again from the sunlight by a foot of ochre-colored scum.

We are not interested in their archeology so I do not know the circumstance which preserved a facade in this way. As their metal softened and gave way—a thing which hastened the war's end—all their buildings gradually collapsed. Perhaps in the final war days this city was sunk by us at the identical time their metal was giving way; whereupon encroaching mud propped up everything along these two city blocks. Future spring-floods will destroy even this temporary, delicate balance.

My oarsmen looked down into this street where once their forebears walked and lived. To my oarsmen the facade was without meaning, was only a shimmering apparition, a thing if either exposed to air or touched by swimmers would collapse in whole sections. As we drifted, the oarsmen did not change expression. They were grateful for this suspended moment of calm, their oars shipped.

By indirection, by other channels, we found the main course of the river. Again the Coxswain's voice drove the oars . . .

Towards noon the next day I saw the first bank-side watch-towers. Then we rowed more slowly, more publicly; first up the tributary, and then steadily between narrow banks of caly.

At the end of a shallow creek, I saw the cliff-face of red earth, the landmark from which the settlement takes its name, "Ochretown."

The rumor of metal had brought me here.

III

Seen from the landing, their town lay motionless beneath its own smoke, a curved, brown river-slug of clay houses. The walls and the roofs of fired-clay shards rose in random tiers between the creek bank and the base of the ochre cliff. Higher, across the cliff-face, I saw their second town: dark, square room-holes, connected by tunnels. In flood time the town moves up the cliff-face and lives miserably until the waters recede.

-You *see* gun?

My counterpart up-river, my Town-Major, had followed me respectfully from the landing to his "Headquarters," and now we were alone in his connected rooms, the walls of pounded earth, one floor covered with muddy rushes. The Town-Major's "desk" was a valuable piece of wood, squared on four sides as though by industrial process, placed trestle-like across fired-clay pedestals. To me the desk symbolized their pathetic reliance on meaningless form; to him, doubtless, the "desk" was a psychic necessity, a holdover from a past when real furniture apparently signified industrial power.

I nodded, Yes. Before starting up-river I had seen gun. Very close in fact *seen.*

-*Osthot?* and my Town-Major leaned across his "desk." Might you have *him.* Now?

To be effective in the Territories, you must understand their *minds.* My Town-Major's enquiry was in part ritualistic, as when more sensitive people make enquiries about personal health, or the weather. For example, "Is *it* happy," or "Is Little Friend asleep?," to them means, "Has the gun lately been discharged? cleaned? oiled? etc." Normally, a Town-Major will not expect each visit to see my gun. With all my counterparts, however, I hold out the possibility of the direct, visual experience.

"Little Friend is *very* near," I said. "He will be happy—sometime—to see light."

-*Osthot?* and my Town-Major placed his hands palm down on the narrow top of his desk, as though to hold on. In many ways he was an able man, but the possibility of seeing it, close-up, caused a visible, almost unbearable, vaguely sexual, tension in his whole body. For all americans there is magic in it; therefore I use their primitive belief for their own self-governance. I now had him ready for business.

"Metal contact, Town-Major. Reported."

-I reported it, Commissioner.

At precisely such moments great administrative restraint with americans is required. I saw two possibilities: the verified on the log in fact was the Town-Major's courier, but profit being the ideological fury of their lives, the man riding the log had assumed the role of informer. Or, when I rowed past the watchtowers, my Town-Major concluded there was a rumor of metal in his enclave.

Effectiveness in the Territories, however, means one is never diverted by *anything* they say. If I had paid an official courier, it was only a cost of governance; if the two men later shared my nominal fee paid unnecessarily, I could admire their tact. All of that I understood, and I do not like it very much for I go by the Manual (as revised):

"You interrogated? Under Section 4?"

From an otherwise able man I got only hyperbole, their eye-rolling "anguish." At the close of a three-minute evasion, I heard the word "Sincere." Always they end lies by "sincere" for it is their signal-word for, "Negative, No."

"I appreciate," and the irony always eludes them, "Your sincerity. Therefore we have work. You and I."

My Town-Major was clearly relieved. Instead of taking a prescribed action, he had called me, by courier, up-river. When he said "sincere," I understood absolutely there was found metal, somewhere.

I stood. Using their own gesture for "action," I slapped my thigh: "Go."

The Town-Major was out the door ahead of me, leading the way.

Above all they like action but they seldom calculate ultimate consequence; to them the going is more important than any policy.

With the Town-Major ahead, with one-half my crew following, we went at a half-trot to the town's edge, then skirted the ochre cliff; by ever-more narrow paths to the north and west, across terrain of rock-face and clay knob, we walked more steeply towards the sun.

Where we went was once a valley. Ahead, stone outcrop marked the ancient ridgeline. Knobs of clay, at this place transformed by wind into grotesque, guardian figures, showed traces of mineral; in crevasses which might trap water the first purple lichens grew.

68

My Town-Major stopped. He signalled the rowers. They sat down beside the path to wait, their heads at rest on their unslung Go-bags.

At the next rise, the trail abruptly stopped.

Below my feet I saw an amphitheatre, a whirlpool-shape of stone two hundred yards across, its walls in past winters scoured by tornado-like winds, falling away—down, down—to the valley floor. What at first seemed empty seat-rows, aisles, and exits were only illusions: sunlight falling across slabs of stone. The Town-Major again pointed to the bottom, the north face.

On stilts, in white relief against granite, I saw an intact section of a poured-concrete freeway. These monumental shards, up-ended in sand, are not unusual; this section, however, was fifty yards long, a black stripe down the centre, an elevated "bridge" leading to and from nowhere. Once a highway of importance ran along the valley floor to one of their cities now gone.

The Town-Major started down the rock face, and I followed.

Finally, at the bottom, my Town-Major stopped. Breathing heavily, perspiring, he leaned with one hand on the smooth, white stilt of the old freeway. We both looked back and up to the rim of the amphitheatre and into the cloudless sky beyond.

-This place, and the Town-Major slapped his thigh. Here they play the game.

I said nothing.

Abruptly the Town-Major turned to the ladder-steps of the concrete stilt and began to climb.

Below him, following carefully, I also climbed.

-Understand Commissioner?

I had patrolled the guardrails of this elevated ruin, kicking debris as I went. The men who discovered this anomoly of wind and stone had returned often to play. The black centre-stripe had become one baseline; stone shards, once almost round, lay everywhere and I saw broken, sun-dried balls of clay. With perhaps nine players of the game on each side, they threw or rolled balls with great force towards improvised, stone "houses"; if a ball went cleanly through a little house, all players of the game could change base, could Go. This elevated "court" was absolutely level, absolutely smooth, a perfect place: I imagined voices of men re-echoing up and across the stone amphitheatre's rim . . .

-*Yako?*

I *yakoed* enough: here was artifact discovery (not reported and here was artifact usage (casual). The rumor of metal had nothing to do with it.

My Town-Major looked away, said nothing.

I expected no answer for every Field Officer and every Town-Major have their little trade-offs, the Manual (as revised) notwithstanding. We both understood playing a game constituted neither recovery of industrial process nor intent to reconstruct. Moreover, next season, the winds might again fill this amphitheatre with blown dust. Nevertheless, in one way, I was annoyed: had my trusted TM and a down-river courier cleverly worked me to buy *this* information? The news of play? No matter, I saw possible leverage in their little exercise; now I might possibly extract a half-levy of men from Ochretown to train as oarsmen . . .

As though reading my thoughts, the Town-Major said,

-Boys, only. Boys play here.

"Osthot?"

-Two boys. Also look. For good ones.

The Town-Major was at the railing. He pointed to narrow pathways along the cliff-face. I understood two players of the game had gone farther and farther up and across the cliff-face looking for "balls."

Because of that, I, too, went into the tunnel of the mine.

As the two boys had come upon an entrance which blended absolutely with a crevasse in the face of the cliff, so did my Town-Major. Climbing up and along the cliff-face, only two steps ahead, my TM seemed to disappear into a shadow. One step more and I, too, was inside: a tunnel, cut with great precision through solid granite. Cool but not dank, wide enough for two, the tunnel led us a quarter of a mile through the steady dark.

As we walked, I thought of my oarsmen now probably asleep in the sun; without them I felt vulnerable for I was up-country, miles from my Headquarters; in the Territory, little tricks up-country are not unknown. Yet even in the dark, I had absolute confidence—and also the gun, the Little Friend . . .

Abruptly our mine shaft ended: we stood in the centre of a vaulted, half-lighted room, a place where four tunnels joined.

The Town-Major clapped his hands.

Sharply the sounds reverberated overhead, then ran away as though on noisy footsteps along the secondary corridors of what once had been one of their mines, possibly for coal.

On the floor of this ominous vault, I saw two parallel ridges of rust: disintegrated rails which led to a larger drift, then probably fell away in a mile of darkness to the wall of silt which blocked an entrance where once men from the old valley assembled to work . . . "Two Boys? Here?" and I imagined first their initial fright and then the reverberation of their echoes at search for stones . . .

-Only two, Commissioner. I have them.

"In regular? In Ochretown?"

-In Special custody.

Special meant the two were isolated-holds, not in the TM's regular cave. In the dark, when he could not see my face well, the Town-Major spoke without evasion: an able man, the kind of verified upon which my Territory depends. If Special-holds, were the boys also kin? Members of an elaborate "family" upon which his own authority in part rested? I cut through all of that:

"*Where* metal?"

Even though he was an american, my Town-Major did not lie:

-Here, Commissioner.

By law the TM could not touch it, but I could touch it, and I did so by kicking.

Fifty yards back along a steeply rising, secondary tunnel, I walked around and around an ugly, low cart. The frame was metal; the corners bolted. The wheels were cast-metal, the rims flanged, the axles machined; front and rear was a hitch; there was a hand-wheel of metal, with a ratchet and cog which once had set the brakes. This find of metal to me was an ugly, repulsive thing. The cart shuddered and rocked in its own rust as I kicked, and kicked, and kicked.

Cars exactly like this, coupled all in a row, once hauled ore or coal to the mine's entrance in the valley. This thing, this rusted scab of their industry, had survived the most successful phase of that long-ago war when the weaponry of my forebears gradually de-tempered all their metal; moreover, this thing had survived all phases of the Metal-Purge Treaties at our war's end. Yet here it was, rotting but whole, disclosed by the play of boys in our own time. Rumors of metal brought me here, and now I had found it: sullen, hibernating in the fetid darkness of a cave . . .

"How many more? These things?"

-No more—now. You *yako,* Commissioner?

My Town-Major was pointing to the round stones which blocked the two, front, flanged wheels of the mine cart.

"No *yako.*"

-Once five, he said patiently. Now *this* one, Commissioner.

I did not like it. One cart to be pulled from a mine, then raised above the amphitheatre walls, then hauled to Ochretown; there, after dark, this thing to be packed in mud, dried, then rafted down-river to a Gulf Base. The terms of the ancient Metal-Purge Treaties hang on.

Worse, the presence of metal made them restless. Even if the packing in mud were done in the Town-Major's restricted enclaves at night, there were always rumors. The americans catch the presence of metal as if catching a disease; soon the metal-disease becomes an epidemic of unrest. Depend on it: secretly they fear it but to touch or to hold metal is their obsession.

-Commissioner: you stand.

My Town-Major motioned me back to the place where the tunnels joined.

In the vaulted room I stood alone. The Town-Major's voice first seemed to whisper. Then his voice rolled along the tunnel from the place in darkness where the cart was:

-*Yako* . . . Ya- K-O . . .! their word which means both to under-stand and to beware.

Like some low-runner, mindless animal the mine cart rattled in the tunnel; it gained speed, a thing long asleep now awakened.

Then it filled the low tunnel mouth, came out growing larger, an apparition of lunging metal . . .

Its front wheels hit two stones. Up the cart leaped, rose slowly, seemed for a moment to float like some hissing, wingless reptile. Half-turning, suspended in shadows above my head, it tilted for-ward, hit on the front trucks, bounced, skidded on a gash of sparks across stone, then end-over-end, disappeared like some wounded, rattling animal into the main shaft, going down.

In darkness it fell end-over-end, the cart shedding wheels, frames, trucks, bouncing on granite until it died against the mine's blocked entrance of silt.

In the silence, I heard one wheel, or one coupling, or a hand-brake rod bounce once, twice along a corridor of granite, and then everything was still. The air of the vault once more became very quiet, as water in a stretch of river becomes quiet after a stone sinks into the mud . . .

-*Now* you understand, Commissioner?

The cart overhead turning in its heavy parabola of flight left me dazed. By saying nothing at all, however, I gave my tacit approval: it was metal gone, and caves bear no witness.

-Rowers. Now we wake them?

I said, "Yes. Back to rowers. Then back to Ochretown."

IV

In spring in my Territory the days are long. When we came back through the town's mudwall gates the sun overhead was half-way towards evening.

My rowers dropped off at the skiff where the other half of my crew was on either side of the up-turned hull putting Go-wax on the planks: their wax makes a "hot" skiff, one more easy to row.

While we had walked back from the cliff and the amphitheatre's rim and now for half an hour in the Town-Major's rooms, his "desk" between us, my TM explained away everything he had not yet done:

Their little game on the freeway ruin was nothing? Agreed. Their search for round stones—not authorized—also was nothing? Agreed. Then two boys found carts coupled all in a row, in a tunnel; not knowing, not ever before having seen cast-metal or flanged wheels or spokes, not ever before having seen hand-wheel brakes or bolts holding two frames, why naturally these things they *no* understand, you *yako,* Commissioner?

Agreed, and now of course the last cart was gone and something like this could never again happen. But I knew the two boys *did* understand. When first they walked around the abandoned carts those things most certainly spoke to them. Embedded in the boy's language, in their legends, in their Myths of Power, of days when water became fire through whirling, dervish-Gods named *Torbeings,* without willing it so, two boys found in wheels and fabricated metal a confirmation of ancient, tribal dreams. Without having to understand they *knew* all carts Go . . .

Either by intent or by lack of enforcement they had touched metal; first the couplings, then a hand-wheel brake; then they probably sat in the cars, as though rowing a boat. Then one day they uncoupled a cart, pushed it a little; the wheels resting on granite turned, moved forward very easily . . . After the first cart lunged out of its tunnel, after it disappeared in a long, industrial gash of sparks, the boys were marked.

After two, after four carts went shrieking away, when only one cart remained, the boys became frightened. At night, at bedtime, they confided to their mothers. Very well I understood: for two boys it was a religious experience, a conversion by metal.

"What action, Town-Major? What *action* you take?"

Suddenly my TM seemed older. I understood: with full-grown men he could have acted under Section 4 (as revised). Down-river my Hearings are absolutely correct, and my Court is Just—or at least no one has ever appealed. Moreover, I understood two boys were valuable, were the hope, were the future of fifty washed-away places like Ochretown. All Town-Majors rule by Theocratic force; their best hope for the town, for the race, is with the young. To invent games, to explore the darkness of tunnels showed early promise; these things I really did understand.

My Town-Major stood.

I followed through corridors. Being of mud and tile, Ochretown had its passages, warrens, stairs, and further passages. All these led upward. I knew the Special holds were in a carved-out room in the other city of the cliff's face, above all flood marks.

The TM motioned for quiet. Stopped.

I stepped up beside him on a raised platform. Together, we looked through a wall-slit and down into a room carved from stone.

In a single ray of sunlight, below, I saw two boys.

Caught motionless in a moment of play, the two looked intently at something. The slant of sunlight touched one boy's face. His cheek was devastatingly white—a blood condition—as though that beautiful forehead had never seen the sun. The face of the second boy was averted, was looking at something between them on the floor. The boy's head raised slightly. For one second the sun blazed like fire on his red hair.

Strangely, I was moved by the sight: young boys, alone, at play in a slant of sunlight.

I stepped down from the platform. At that moment, for me, this case was closed; aside, I whispered to my Town-Major, "Now, if they are clean, TM. Or, if they are your kin. Or if . . ."

Coldly, the Town-Major stared at me. Also whispering, he wished me to know they were indeed of his wife's family—but very distantly related. Very.

With new resolve the Town-Major went back to the observation platform. I joined him for I wished to look down again, to see two boys at play in sunlight.

Now they stood apart.

On the floor between them, I saw their very accurate model: a replica of the mine cart. Unmistakably it was so: axles, sides, a twig for the handbrake rod, dried-clay wheels.

As I watched through the slit, the boy with red hair drew back his arm. On sun-baked wheels the little cart bumped once, then went wobbling, but very straight, as though on rails, went straight across the floor; and it carried truly its small load of small pebbles into the white-faced boy's waiting hand.

The boys laughed. In their reechoing voices I heard the joy of invention with this new thing which they had made.

V

Down-river, past nightfall, the breeze was warm and our skiff slid hot between mudbanks; for one moment, all in a row, the tips of the oars caught the first moonlight.

What happened in Ochretown really was by the Manual (revised): I did my job conscientiously; the Town-Major did his. At the same time, however, the way he "managed" me illustrates both their national obsession and the reason no two days in the OMT are ever the same.

When we looked down into the Special-hold room, when I saw their small cart run on wheels of clay, for one long, attenuated moment my Town-Major said nothing at all. Then without hesitation, as though he saw something clearly, he turned and went back along the corridors.

Soon my TM came back, this time with two clay bowls of porridge, which was the late-afternoon meal. Through a smaller slit near the floor the Town-Major pushed the bowls into their room.

Unseen, silent, we watched from above: the boys ate their porridge. Greedily, they licked the bowls. Then they caused the bowls to run slowly on the rims: two wheels going in ever-smaller circles on the floor.

Patiently, we watched. In a little while the two boys became tired of this play; they laid down side-by-side as though to sleep. Because the cereal was drugged in the usual way, the boys soon were very much asleep in each other's arms—but were still breathing lightly.

Together we went into their cell. With my river boot I ground the clay-model cart and the wheels and the hand-brake into powder— a gesture. True, with the clay beneath my foot, I felt I had done something which was in some way disproportionate; at the same time it was a symbolic thing, a gesture for the benefit of my Town-Major.

Possibly my Town-Major also felt he should prove himself symbolically; or perhaps at that moment he wished to try my loyalty to him; or—more probably—it really is their obsession. In any event, he said almost patiently,

-*Now* you show Little Friend the sunlight? You *yako?*

Because we were alone, because very much I need the loyalty of all Town-Majors; because my trust in him was great; yes, and to confirm his own correct action in this case, I took from my concealed holster one of the two extant firearms in this entire Territory. One of my authorized pistols is at my Headquarters, well secured; the other firearm now rested lightly in my hand.

The Town-Major reached out his hand. He touched the gun.

I watched his face contort. His eyes became wide, startled, and then he smiled by drawing back his lips until—convulsively—he laughed.

Without having to be shown, without heitation, as though all of his life it had been waiting for this, had remembered its role from some primordial, industrial past, the Town-Major's finger curled, found the trigger, and—by instinct—pulled.

Nothing happened.

Nothing happened until he was first above the boy with the pale face, and then legs astraddle above the boy with the red hair. Neither boy knew it or felt anything when I showed my TM an ultimate thing: a safety catch, how to press it, how to make the blue, loaded revolver . . . how to make it. Go.

In what manner the Town-Major disposed of two bodies and which details he told their mothers, I do not know.

In about three weeks, without having to ask, I received a half-levy of men from Ochretown; although their language is not known either to me or to my Coxswain, he feels—given time—they will become very good oarsmen.

Allegedly these men were taken from beyond my present Territory, from a valley where all through the night giant kilns throw flames of lavender and yellow against the low-hanging clouds. There being no rumors of metal, however, I shall neither seek that valley nor climb their escarpments of white, pure clay which are said to rear skyward somewhere to the West.

I was half-asleep but sitting upright when my Coxswain raised the first winking torch on our landing. Soon I saw the higher, bank-side lights of my own Headquarter windows reflecting all in a row on the waters of a river which seems never to end.

The Architect's Wife

Only for a second and too late he knew he was falling because when cannon-shaped rolls of blueprints and the edge of the drafting table for one instant were at eye level, when sunlight from the oblong, high architect's windows slanted down through the cross-braces and the trestle legs of a table and down into his eyes, when his body struck the waxed tiles of the floor and let go all its separate parts, only then, after the paper and wood and plastic shapes of their office went past his face like some composite, liquid, apparition, did he feel the chest pain, and then he felt—nothing at all.

II

"It's simply too soon."

Although the architect's wife had driven quickly from their home, and although she had cried a little while she waited in the corridor at Dominican for their family doctor to arrive from the club, she was now focused, and attentive, and ready to know more. She understood unless she was all right herself they would not admit her to the intensive care ward at all. But because this was Fred's doctor, their family doctor, and also a tennis player, she expected to find out about everything.

"Also, Joyce, we are lucky on this one," and the family doctor's voice was vibrant with good management for he had come in to Dominican through another entrance, and had gone at once to the intensive care ward and the thing to do now was to emphasize the positive aspects. Fred's age, yes. Also Fred probably was in above-average shape? Also the proximity of the architectural offices to Dominican and the promptness of the ambulance service—probably a new record—since the ambulance was by chance gassing up at the Shell station across the street. And finally: Doctor Eric Battner, the specialist, just by chance on this Wednesday was in the hospital. These things were all favorable. A really big tilt for Fred.

The architect's wife said, Yes, for Dr. Battner was a well-known local specialist, and was in the ward with another patient. Yes, because she was educated and a mother and had worked once for Army Personnel. The architect's wife saw for herself that all these things were very favorable.

"Then would you *say,* is the whole thing severe? Will Fred be all right? Won't he?

The family doctor understood Joyce was an intelligent woman, so he told her almost everything. But: the big thing is the resources of the patient, right? From long practice, he avoided overt promises.

"I'll say this: right now Fred is in awfully good hands. Here at Dominican. Right?" And then he added what he believed to be a more personal touch, "After all, Freddie designed our new house, and it's real fine. Now all of us simply have to wait."

In the ward for intensive care what she saw was each bed in a separate bay, the beds and the unit itself shaped like a four-leaf clover, and each bed with its electrical connections leading to the nurse's monitor panel: a fantasy of rubber-tube vines criss-crossing against sunlight, the suck and gurgle and the *tick-tick-tick* of totally supportive machinery. Seeing all of these things at once, seeing the mechanics of it, but not at once recognizing the bundle harnessed between sheets really was Fred, all this made the wife's arms and then her shoulders come unfastened. When she crumpled only the print-fabric of her dress for a moment seemed to contain her.

As the wife fell against his chest, the family doctor very expertly put his own hands beneath her arms. As he lowered her to the couch, the doctor was also motioning with his head for the Duty Nurse: come here! And bring something for this one . . .

"Now you are feeling better," the family doctor said, after the wife had smelled the ammonia and had drunk more water. At the sound of his good voice, the Architect's wife remembered. She sat upright on the couch.

She looked once more across the ward to the place her husband was enmeshed in the tubes of rubber and the electrical cords. "Seeing Fred. Like that . . .

"'Look," the Doctor told her. "Any heart attack is almost

exactly like this. In the organ itself a little artery lets go. Then it clots. Heals itself . . . you see . *Then,* say in about forty-eight hours, that little branch either holds or it breaks off and we get another so-called attack. Then that little branch clots, and heals. That's how these cases get better.''

"Always?''

"Fred's young. He's real athletic . . .''

The wife thought of a stretched tennis net, of white lines intersecting on a court of clay, of a tennis racquet aloft in Fred's hand, slicing sunshine and air, getting back into shape to play the Couples Competition.

"Fred is only thirty-seven!''

"That old? Well, it does happen. To all of us.''

"Didn't you hear? Anything? At his last check-up?'' and because all the wives of all his patients said things like this, the family physician gave not so much a correct answer as he gave a correct, general, response.

"Nothing showed up—and that's also perfectly normal.''

"Oh?'' and at this moment those wives who cared a very great deal always began to blame themselves, so the family doctor then dealt with that attitude.

"Joyce, we have to accept one thing: neither of us could have done anything. These things happen.''

"I see,'' but if there was no blame on anyone at all, if these things simply happened, then why did it happen at two o'clock on a Wednesday in the partnership's new architectural offices, at exactly the moment Fred was about to shake hands at the door with the Vice President from Esso, just as Fred was saying goodbye to a really very important, potential client?

III

At first the architect did not fully realize two days had passed and yet he understood he had dreamed for a second that he was about to awake; then he opened his eyes and waited for a minute and then took inventory of each separate part of his body. He was awake. Yes.

The architect observed closely the design details of the window sash, the shape of the light beam slanting down into the ward, the cross-hatch outlines of other beds. In the background he heard the even, escaping breath of the other patients, all of them held in rubber-tube vines, held motionless by wires and plugs, the harnessed diligence, the absolute routine of an intensive care ward.

When the nurse did not come to his bedside, the architect concluded no one at all was for the moment actually on duty in this enclave of the hospital. He thought of the landscape beyond the windows, of the familiar California county-seat town at three o'clock in the morning; cumulus clouds aloft, upland the low hills where they had built the tennis club; to the south the Bay, and the sea beyond.

In precise architectural detail, he recalled their firm's Mall Project—curbs, gutters, arbors, seats—the new centre of town. Also the airport runway-extensions, backed by the merchants and professional men alike. These things were a composite of his own life: things of wood, of poured concrete, built to Code, useful for commerce, necessary for progress, projects which sometimes took their first real life at the firm's drafting tables, were later lived in, used . . .

The vision of new construction beneath moonlight and the professional knowledge about State Fire Laws and Exits to ground-floor levels caused the architect to think, "Why I will do that!" Drive on out to their own house, and there touch the familiar light switch just at the left of a very finely conceived and executed entrance and door, and in that way enter in the customary way and slide into bed with his wife as he had done in years past when at all hours of the morning he came home from the firm's offices, after a job was ready for the Oslid. Of the three partners, he was the one who could work best all through the night and still come back to the office to supervise at the regular time. Reserves, they said, of nervous energy.

His slacks and his shoes were in the small storage locker at the head of the bed: the locker itself was the kind of detail some other good architect had designed for exactly these moments.

He opened the balcony door. In the warm, sibilant California night air he breathed deeply, and then walked very quickly down the fire-escape steps, and through low shrubbery, and into the parking lot beyond.

In moonlight, as though viewed from aloft, the landscape was a vast, unrolled, unfinished map: hedge-rows and lot lines and the rows of boulevard lights to the east; towards the valley, three roads crossed, and beyond lay the grid-work of fields. The unrolled, unfinished landscape seemed to breathe in and then give back the light to the enormous, slate-grey hemisphere of sky overhead.

The architect drove towards home. The side streets, the drug-store signs of neon were familiar, remembered. The street suddenly curved outward, and around. At the curve's widest arc he saw the view-point, an engineered slab of clay which seemed to hang in the moonlight above a new, strange perspective. At the town's edge, where the countryside below receded stubbornly down in a series of outcrops until woods and sky and the valley floor became a single slab of darkness. The architect stopped the car near the guard rail to view what was vacant, or built on, or awaiting development.

In the moonlight, one foot on the guardrail, he seemed to hear the industrial noises he knew so well: behind him, perhaps in the centre of the town, near the freight yards, again and again he heard the re-echo of a black, iron, demolition ball swinging implacably against old circus posters on walls of brick. Then it was the earth mover's engine, the yelp of tempered steel against boulders in hard-pan, the roll of water and gravel and cement inside a Redi-Mix drum. Good sounds, the machinery he loved; yet, with the trained part of his architect's mind which was so subtly adjusted to fact, he thought, "Probably no, probably only the sound of wind through office buildings. Union men would not be worked this late because of overtime . . ."

Directly below the guard rails a new project was under construction, a job in town not at all known to him. This was strange for his life was completely with design, and design implied construction; secretly, he prided himself on knowing in the whole county what was currently being financed, or ready for building. If a permit was issued, he knew about it. And yet here were earth-movers and power shovels, the metal irridescent in the moonlight, ready to move when the whistle blew . . .

From above the outlines of this—in fact—major project were clear: apparently single units, each unit of seven single-storey houses connected by a mall to a centre two-storey place. Each unit was like the spokes of a wheel. The whole project was a dozen laid-down wheels, informally adjacent, in different stages of completion. To the East, the first wheels were already under roof, stuccoed, and landscaping planted; West, the units were only framed. In the farthest shadows beneath Cottonwood trees, he saw only utility trenches, and stakes, and piled-up drain tile and lumber. Seen together, the separate small houses, the centre buildings, the connecting malls, was exciting. But the architectural firm, the contractor, or the overall purpose, even the general intention eluded his mind.

The old man touched the architect's shoulder.

In the moonlight, in the way of strangers who by chance are bound in an overwhelming, mutual interest, they began to talk about the project below.

Being a watchman, the old man said, "You bet. Easier to keep an eye on the whole show from up here, on the ramp . . ." and that's why he had walked up, for the height, and had also noted the automobile headlights with possibly a driver who smoked for most especially fire was the real hazard. That's why he viewed it all at once about every other hour. A big job for sure, and not half worked-out, they said. So naturally wouldn't the watchman side of it last through the winter months, unforeseen circumstances permitting?

Together they walked past moon-drenched footings, and steel reinforcing rods; then through a connecting street to an adjacent wheel of buildings where the framing and duct work was a crosshatch of black bars against the sky. Still talking, the old man guided their steps across curbs and around piles of gyp-board, and through an arched, low, opening in a wall.

"This opening calls for a real big gate," the older man said, and with the gate the unit was finished except for carpet shipped by truck from Georgia, and mis-routed, and no doubt lost right now on some loading dock in Buffalo, New York . . ."

"A retirement community, you said?"

"For real elderly folks," the night watchman said, himself formerly a Teamster, lately retired.

"Look at it this way," the architect said, "They have a core building at the centre of each 'wheel'. That's your social, psychic, and *security* function for each complex," and it followed, simply in terms of design, that from the centre office the many windows permitted social monitoring of the single-storey dwellings. Thus the Elderly could look towards a vital, supportive, two-storey core, and thus a sense of community would gradually prevail, with the requisite stability, and capable of a wide spectrum of personal adjustment. And besides, this design also provides for maximum mobility, as the tenant elects. Each social unit, of course, may have cooperative, supportive ventures with its "neighbor" . . .

The night watchman said, "Yup", and although he had not studied the blueprints, it certainly was a big job and a rumor going around among the carpenter gangs that the whole thing might be doubled in size.

The implication of an even larger construction budget excited the architect in an old, familiar way.

"You know this project embodies an old, very successful, 18th Century idea of the Charnel House, probably the most practical socialization to date of the very *human* problem of growing old . . ."

Although the architect did not say it either to the watchman or to the open utility trenches, a further outline, a larger presentation—possibly to a potential client or to a financier—came to his mind: "Furthermore, gentlemen, our contained social units, our 'hub and spoke' concept presents a sympathetic managerial centre; a focus for accounts and collections; an overall tone which is benign . . ."

These thoughts brought forth others. His mind raced ahead. The architect surrendered to his own vision, and liked what he saw.

"I will take you on across," and the night watchman, head bowed, lead the architect across a plank above the widest open ditch on the project. Beneath the plank bridge lay a long line of unconnected, disjointed cast-concrete pipes which led onward to the row of Cottonwoods in moonlight.

When the architect was once more standing in the moonlight beside his own automobile he felt a terrible, saw-tooth of regret.

It was true: beyond the overall concept of hub and spoke, beyond the small elegant details of arches and gates and malls with flower beds, beyond the overall "Spanish" tone, for the first time in his life the architect felt an uncontestable sense of regret.

As the first breeze before the first light of still another day touched the town to which he had given so much of his professional life, he saw the ghostly, illuminated project was precisely the thing which he, himself, should have conceived, the thing he, himself, should have carried through to a stunning conclusion. This feeling of regret intersected exactly with what had always been his secret seldom articulated compassion for the elderly, the very old, for those people now alone, or abandoned, with not much money, the children gone, and their only alternative the isolation of house trailers, with no one to care towards the end of a life perhaps useful, or merely finished.

At last the architect seemed to have found a thing both socially significant and also practicable: here was a design absolutely at the service of humanity, and precisely called for by the times. In retrospect, it was the sort of thing he had always really wanted to do. By comparison the single-family dwellings for doctors, the runway extensions for industry, the Mall for the City now seemed either trivial or merely cosmetic. At a deeper, more emotional level, he felt this vision of a project also represented exactly the kind of place that he, himself, would go and would stay in until the end when everything—when Joyce and the boys and their present home beyond the city's edge—when all other things were past, were gone.

And he faced it: the regret was tinged with a self-pity, with envy: some other architect had carried through this great, good project, this stuff of architectural fame, of influence in the world at large, in ages to come. Yes, and shame: all of their public, partnership designs in the end were always compromised. He remembered the church which caused a parish quarrel—and was not paid for yet; the three schools with their crippled financing, political wrangles, and too much plywood; and all their jobs, no matter where, thwarted by outmoded State and Federal specs, and fire laws more than a half-century old. By contrast the architect saw for a moment the possiblity that his concept a community for the old could be in fact free of either public compromise or the shoddiness of merely private efficiency.

But he would, the architect told himself. Yes, he would. And as he got back into the car and switched on the engine he said to himself he really would come back here to observe this thing. And after that—gradually—he would renounce his role in the partnership's office as the man who always got the job done—no matter at what personal cost. Once free, he would devote vision and total energy to projects like this for the benefit of every man and woman over— say—sixty-two years of age.

As the architect backed the car and then drove quickly away from the guard rails and the viewpoint, he felt if he now steered straight ahead, he would almost at once intersect with a familiar, well-lighted boulevard. After that, south. Then the turn-off into their newer development where every house was appreciating every day, the acreage itself at one time an old olive grove . . . And then their own driveway.

And his wife would be waiting and it would be as everything had always seemed to be all of the days of his life.

V

Before noon the architect's wife was called back to the hospital. Now she waited in this cubicle as the nurse had directed and she saw there were no books on the shelves and no window to the outside. California sunshine: only a small couch, two chairs, and a low, useless table. And no: not yet possible to see the patient; and no: not possible even for members of the immediate family.

The abstract, guarded tone of the nurse's directions caused the architect's wife to think of falling. But the thought only passed through her mind and with all the strength in the muscles of her legs and with some other inward strength she held herself erect. It was as though she had grasped and had held to a slanting edge of sunlight coming through the venetian blinds and only in that way had been able to reply, "Of course. I'll wait in here."

For the moment there was nothing at all to do except to close out the past: a sleepless night, her two small boys at home; the reasonable, yet unpaid bills in this morning's mail; the partner's wives and their well-intended casseroles. To these things she implacably denied consideration in order to focus on what the nurse had suggested, were, "recent developments".

"Now in Fred's case," and again it was their family doctor—tennis partner and client—who took care of them all.

"He's worse? Isn't he?" for while waiting the architect's wife concluded on her own that if Fred were in fact improved, if in fact everything were really all right, then the nurse would not have been quite so firm, not quite so anxious, to get a member of the immediate family out of the corridor and into this cubicle, no doubt a space designed by some other architect for exactly this purpose, where the immediate family watied to hear news which was not entirely good.

The doctor did not answer her directly but went on to say that in these cases the prognosis—how it might come out—was not always easy to state. Much depended—as suggested at the beginning—on the total resources of the patient.

"I see. Fred really is only thirty-seven. Don't cardiacs come much later? Usually?"

Actually the family doctor was now estimating the wife's own strength, her own resources.

"Noooo, Joyce. Not precisely. Now in Fred's case . . ." and he went on to review the rationale of all intensive care; then the actual management of all such cases; and what in the first crucial thirty-six hours or so had reflected in their tests.

"Fred really is not good?" and then she added, "As we had hoped?"

"That's why I called Dr. Battner back to this case. In fact, Battner is with Fred now. But . . ."

Very suddenly the architect's wife stood up. She was going into the Ward. To his bedside. To see . . . As she stepped around the useless coffee table, as she almost got her hand as far as the door, that door opened. It was Dr. Battner.

Because the two doctors had only to exchange that particular look and because they had both known since before noon how this one was going to come out, the younger doctor said, "Dr. Battner's here. He will tell you. The latest."

When the door closed the family physician was gone and the architect's wife looked directly at the specialist.

"I think the two of us had best sit down. Right here," and in this way the older man put her under the yoke of his prescriptive, wary voice; the architect's wife almost gladly did what she was told to do.

After the specialist considered the evidence of her sleepless, tear-stained face as against the firmness of her voice, he concluded she was not ready to hear it.

"We did absolutely everything, Joyce. And in fact—early on— we even got a few minor breaks. But . . ."

She looked at the older doctor first with disbelief, and then with amazement—and finally—acceptance, "Oh, oh!" and then she said, "My god . . . my god!" even though neither she nor Fred had gone to church. "Ohhhh . . ."

When she neither stood nor went exactly into shock and in fact when he observed that this news was not entirely unexpected, the doctor said what he could.

"Joyce, it's tragic. Fred had a really massive experience in his office. Usually we have a lull, a kind of recuperation period. And then. Well, last night he suffered a third attack.''

She nodded. The little arteries in his heart had not mended, had not healed themselves, not after all . . .

"After that last one. Well, his heart didn't have anything left. At all.''

"But why. He was so creative. He had some really wonderful projects in mind. He was going to . . .''

"The *why* of it?'' and the older doctor always felt it odd that so many of the wives asked the identical question. Nevertheless he always gave an opinion on each case, and especially to those who were young. He admired the architect's wife: a fine beautiful young woman with a great many useful years ahead . . .

"Joyce, I don't know your husband's total medical history. No one does; such a history cannot exist. So we speculate—and not much more. Perhaps this was a genetic thing, somewhere back in the family line. There are contributing factors in the kind of life which all of us lead. Tension. Diet. Cigarettes—I imagine he smoked. And architects are like some doctors in some ways—myself included.'' And then as though to conceal nothing at all from her the older doctor turned his scrubbed, specialized, very professionally trained hands upward for her inspection, as though to convey to her that there were no secrets to conceal. None.

She thought of the two small boys at home, being watched by— and she couldn't even remember the woman's name. And if this were in the family line, and in the life we all lead, then in years ahead she saw herself as an old woman sitting again in this same cubicle, being told about her sons.

Suddenly the architect's wife put all past and all future things from her mind. Suddenly she seemed to bring all of her background and her education and her personal courage to bear on a single moment. She had realized that Dr. Battner had other cardiac patients. They, too, would now need his time.

As though this precise moment had been anticipated from time-past when mankind began, as though this came to her down the corridors, the dim never-ending architecture of the Race, a thought came to her mind, a thing she instantly recognized as necessary and therefore to be totally believed, something she could cling to and would repeat to their wide circle of friends and even later to her own sons when they, themselves, were old enough to ask her what

89

had happened:

"So he did not suffer. Felt no pain."

"No, of course not," the older doctor said, even though very little was known about the total, cumulative effect of massive sedation. Nevertheless, he also recognized this was one belief, held in common, which allowed both of them to stand.

By herself, the architect's wife took the first step toward the nearest telephone, towards the exit steps of the hospital, and into the wide, noble design of the world and the projects of men: to those completed, or now being built, or to come.

The Executive Touch

ALLIED HIDE & SPECIALTY CO., INC.
1 TANNERY ROW
PENNINGTON, ILLINOIS

20 March 1972

(Mrs.) Barbara Blakey
2223 Country View Terrace
Pennington, Illinois

My Dear Barbara:

This letter conveys my heartfelt condolences to you, to
Ed's immediate family in California, and to your boys who
probably do not fully understand all that has happened.
Enclosed, also, are three checks which pertain to your late
husband's all too tragic severance from ALLIED H & S.

First, Barbara, I want you to know all of us felt the
funeral ceremonies were exactly right: dignified, tasteful,
well managed. The large, non-Company "town" attendance
confirmed Ed's value to our little community. I, myself,
had not fully realized the extent of his personal involvement:
Indian Guides, Little League, and no less than three Pennington
service clubs, including Rotary of which he was past-president.
These organizations will miss Ed Blakey's cheerful affirmative
presence. To me, Ed's "outside" interests again underscored
the vital role of our company executives in bringing forth
good community relations. In Pennington, this was not always
the case. Also, I hope you think one big AH & S "All-Employees"

blanket of carnations entirely appropriate and not an hour passes that I do not ask the searching question, "How shall AH & S ever replace our good soldier Ed Blakey?"

Why our Lockheed "Lodestar" crashed in West Virginia only a few miles from our newest tannery remains a mystery. The government team and our more flexible Flight-ops group under A. K. Carver are still investigating. No doubt the unexpected change in local, mountainous weather contributed. In any event, Barbara, AH & S maintenance work is always well in excess of minimum FAA standards. Those of us who also flew regularly in line of duty had the greatest confidence in both the Lockheed and her crew. Personally, I doubt if the whole story will ever be known. Given the facts, I suppose we must accept the accident as one of life's necessary, tragic happenings.

The three checks enclosed are for you and your sons. The first check covers Ed's full month's salary (and allowances) even though the airplane crashed on 5th March. The second check of $15,000.00 will come as a pleasant surprise. Ed did not know it, but two years ago, I contracted an "Accidental Death in Flight" program--at no cost to company personnel. You and your family are beneficiaries of this company foresight. In addition, a third check of $4,000.00 is an administrative token of appreciation, a bonus for Ed's past services. My personal wish is that this amount be dedicated to the future education of your two sons. I hope you agree.

Meanwhile, I understand you will stay on in Pennington. I hope you will keep in touch. If problems arise, do not hesitate to call on me, just as though I were in fact a God-father to Robbie and Mark. Oh yes, I nearly forgot to mention a minor item: two checks carry "Waiver Certificates" which are self-explanatory; our legal counsel routinely requires this sort of endorsement in all such cases.

Very sincerely yours,

J. KELLY JOHNS
President, and General Manager

Blind carbon copies to:
- Maurice Cohen, Finance
- Hack Bronson, Legal

ALLIED HIDE & SPECIALTY CO., INC.
1 TANNERY ROW
PENNINGTON, ILLINOIS

20 March 1972

(Mrs.) Gustave Lyons
R.F.D. Box 113
Millburgh, Illinois

Dear Mary:

It now being two weeks since the funeral I send my personal
condolences. Enclosed find two (2) checks to cover your
husband's terminal pay and allowances with AH & S for which
he flew so many years.

I regret sincerely I could not attend Gus's funeral services
at the United Methodist in Millburgh. Unfortunately, without
consultation, Ed Blakey's services were scheduled here in
Pennington at the same hour. I felt a prior obligation to
accompany Mrs. Blakey and her two young boys to their father's
funeral. I did, however, get out to Millburgh and personally
left the Company's "All-Employees" spray of roses at the
funeral home. Although less personal, I believe the closed-
casket procedure was the best thing because all our men were
pretty well bruised in the crash. In any event, I was with
you at Millburgh in spirit.

The two checks enclosed are for you. The first check
covers Gus's regular two-week pay period (and allowances)
even though the airplane crashed on 5th March. The second
check of $10,000.00 will come as a pleasant surprise. Gus
did not know it, but two years ago I contracted an ADIF
program--at no cost to company personnel. You are the beneficiary
of this company foresight. I hope this little lift will
provide additional financial security for you in the years
ahead. Oh yes, I nearly forgot one minor item: the two
checks carry "Waiver-Certificates" which are self-explanatory;
our legal counsel routinely requires this sort of endorsement
in all cases of termination.

As regards the probable causes of the crash, I can add
nothing to what you have already read in the local newspaper.
Company maintenance procedures are always well above minimum
FAA requirements; unforeseen weather conditions all across
Appalachia doubtless were a contributing factor. Probably
we shall never know the precise truth.

In conclusion, I want you to know that all of us are going
to miss Old Gus up there in the left seat of the Lodestar.
He was a superb pilot; he knew the Lockheed well. Always

cheerful, cooperative, and a fine man in every way, the
Company will not soon find his replacement. Gus will be
missed. I understand he was born and raised near Millburgh.
I hope you think it fitting he should be laid to rest in the
family plot.

Feel free to consult with me personally on any problems
which may arise.

Sincerely yours,

J. KELLY JOHNS
President, and General Manager

bcc: Finance & Legal

94

ALLIED HIDE & SPECIALTY CO., INC.
1 TANNERY ROW
PENNINGTON, ILLINOIS

20 March 1972

(Mrs.) Ralph Shambrough
c/o Mr. Art Henderson, Apt. 12
5000 S. W. 59th Terracette
South Miami, Florida

Dear Mrs. Shambrough:

This letter conveys my heartfelt personal condolences to
you and to Ralph's immediate family. Also, I enclose two
checks.

First, however, let me state that I agreed wholeheartedly
with your decision to leave Pennington immediately after the
funeral services. It was very considerate of Mr. Henderson,
Ralph's old friend from cadet days, to bring his trailer to
Illinois in order to move your household goods to his apartment
in Miami. You are young. You will soon make a new life for
yourself in--I confess--a more interesting area than Pennington,
Illinois.

Although in his first civilian job Ralph flew only a six-.
month probationary period for AH & S, he was well-liked,
always cheerful, and showed great promise as a "Flying Executive."
Although only twenty-eight years old, Ralph had excellent
military (jet) experience and already had lived a full,
exciting life. He brought a new military alertness and tone
to our whole aircraft operation. He will be missed.

The check enclosed is for you. The check covers Ralph's
regular pay as of March 5. Included also is a Company-paid
ADIF insurance check for $6,000.00 which will come as a
pleasant surprise. You will note a self-explanatory "Waiver-
of-Claims" certificate on the reverse of the check to be
signed upon deposit.

I hope these tokens of our appreciation for Ralph's past
services help you across the rough spots ahead.

Yours truly,

J. KELLY JOHNS
President, and General Manager

JKJ:gjp

MEMORANDUM

C O N F I D E N T I A L

TO: Sheldon Thomas, Vice President, Personnel

Dear Shell--

This Memorandum (CONFIDENTIAL) in part confirms our prior
discussion as regards replacements for: 1) Ed Blakey; 2)
the two Lodestar pilots.

1.   RE NEW SALES MANAGER:

Now I don't want to imply anything bad about the deceased,
but let's learn something from the facts. Namely, our new
Sales Manager must:

a.   Must <u>know</u> all product lines from our twelve tanneries,
     through our finish-plants and right on to final customer
     satisfaction. Blakey didn't. That's why I kept putting
     his ass on our airplanes, to get him out of Pennington
     and <u>to</u> <u>our</u> <u>production</u> <u>centers</u>.

b.   Must show 101 percent loyalty to AH & S management.
     Blakey didn't. More than once I asked him directly
     how much <u>company</u> <u>time</u> his Indian Guides, Little League
     and/or Rotary was costing me. I won't bore you with
     his justifications; I state unequivocally that Ed
     Blakey lacked a sense of proportion.

c.   Must be <u>cost</u> <u>and</u> <u>profit</u> <u>conscious</u>. Blakey wasn't. I
     grant his figures always <u>looked</u> good but the sales-
     costs for his so-called "Incentive Program for Excellence"
     contributed more to his personal popularity in the
     field than it put pure cowhide profits on our ledgers.
     In short, all of us carried both him <u>and</u> his "incentive"
     concepts. He was lucky to be so well known in Pennington--
     which is a very, <u>very</u> small town.

Finally, I want to see final interviews with young, aggressive,
straight <u>men</u> who won't whine and bitch just because it's a weekend
and the weather is a little sour over West Virginia.   On
practically every flight this past three months, I practically
ordered Blakey to get on the Lodestar. A man that won't fly
anyplace at any time won't...well...anything.

Looking ahead: we will recruit a replacement <u>outside</u> AH & S:
<u>do</u> <u>not</u> <u>promote</u> <u>from</u> <u>within</u>. That way we would only get another
<u>Blakey</u>, small-bore.

As a matter of courtesy, I will ask Mr. Oaker for his New York recommendations. He owns other industrial interests and he gets around in both production and merchandising circles. I attach my own list of possible replacements. You may want to contact any or all of them in a preliminary way. I already gave you my new lower salary range for the job. Fringe as negotiated, of course.

Now: let's get our new man aboard in thirty (30) days. A good Jew who knows leather might be the ticket, but no Californians. Not again!

2. RE NEW PILOT REPLACEMENTS:

Pretty much accept Carver's recommendations on replacements. Again, we can learn something from the facts.

Gus was all right, but not much of an instrument pilot. He was Senior pilot because in the old days he walked out of the cornfield to fly a single-engine Fairchild for the previous company owners--well before my time. We paid him plenty for sloppy flying, a "know-it-all," taciturn attitude which some customers found not easy to take. And all of us were aware of his drinking habits. At the very least our new Senior must be able to say "Sir" to a potential buyer without making it a Supreme Court case re discrimination.

Looking ahead: we will promote from our present list, at an appropriate salary savings (commensurate with Carver's judgment). In addition, our new man should have the potential of Executive Leadership and the ability to take over from A. K. Carver, if it comes to that.

Re: Shambrough. No comment.

We might pick up a well-trained youngster who has been laid-off by United or TWA. If he's local to Pennington, so much the better. No military types, please.

On balance, I see this terrible accident gives us a chance to restudy our basic concepts (and costs) of AH & S versus Utilization of Executive Aircraft.

Okay, let's crank it up.

Cordially,

J. K. J.

97

MEMORANDUM

C O N F I D E N T I A L   and   H A N D   D E L I V E R

TO: Maurice Cohen, Vice President, Finance

Dear Murray:

I dictate this at midnight, trying to clean up the mess of
5 March. Here are some suggestions and facts (CONFIDENTIAL
and HAND DELIVER) on the financial aspects.

1. ACCIDENTAL DEATH IN FLIGHT PROGRAM WITH EQUITY
    INDEMNITY (recap):

From prior conversations and Voucher Request Forms, you
know my decision on reimbursing next-of-kin was as follows:

Blakey $19,000.00
      NB: in two checks, one ostensibly
      for an "education" program.
Gus Lyons 10,000.00
      NB: no minor children now alive
Shambrough 6,000.00

TOTAL   35,000.00

Since our specially negotiated contract with Equity Indemnity
was to insure any and all (undesignated) company personnel
aboard (maximum $250,000 per occurence) at $40,000.00 per
head, AH & S will collect $120,000.00 and no questions asked.
Thus, we take down a favorable balance on this item of $85,000.

Murray, I hope there is some way you can reflect that
amount as operating profit in the current year. I could use
it for--as you know--wholesale hide prices are killing us.

2. LOCKHEED "LODESTAR" N-770 (recap):

I can be brief about that turkey: Legal confirms your
suggestion of the revised depreciation concept. That's a
break. Good work. On insurance, Legal advises we are free
and clear on any so-called reimbursement at alleged "fair-
market value." So we go for the whole amount, and no questions
asked.

Our coverage also has a provision for on-board added equipment.
Since Gus burned it all on the side of a mountain, let's
confirm that everything reasonable was "aboard." Two such

items: first, A. K. Carver had purchased some fancy new radio nagivational gear, but--as is increasingly usual with him--had not yet got the stuff installed in the Lockheed. Let's say all of it was installed, even though you have to predate a Work Order if questioned. Since we will never buy another Lodestar, let's cash-out that specialized gear now. Secondly, let's claim Blakey took with him on that last trip quite a few of his fancy sales-promotion kits-- which he may have, for all I know. AH & S has plenty of cowhides tied up in that fancy little project and I strongly suspect our replacement sales manager had damned well better have some fresh approaches to a great many things around here. So let's peddle a few of those kits to the insurance carrier. You handle it.

Looking ahead: I have had two opinions about our Operations (Aircraft): first, the Lockheed was about all Gus could handle. Therefore, Carver allowed the sub-qualifications of one man to hinder a necessary company upgrading of our total flight Operation. Furthermore, we have been disappointed about the high maintenance costs on the Locky, not forgetting the fact that Carver actually wanted to replace both engines (Dallas Airmotive).

Secondly, our very tragic accident of the 5th of March now allows us to consider the question of a possible upgrading of the quality of all AH & S Executive Aircraft.

You have my Memorandum to A. K. Carver on this important issue.

I permit myself to say the following: A. K. Carver had better see this juncture in AH & S Operations (Aircraft) as an opportunity. At last, we need not bend our mature, managerial judgments to a situation we inherited from a previous, local, family-owned, two-horse tannery.

3. AIRCRAFT ACCIDENT AND AH & S LIABILITY (Recap):

Legal worked up an appropriate "Waiver-of-Claim Certificate" for the reverse side of all next-of-kin checks. Legal doubts if such waivers are worth a damn in court but they may discourage plaintiff actions.

Legal is also of the opinion (I do not agree) that the Blakey woman might have a case, especially before a Pennington jury, on the grounds that I knew for a fact that the weather was sour, extraordinary late hour of departure, etc. Apparently the pilots have no case at all for either they contributed negligence or they failed to exercise due caution.

I expect no static.

You received carbon copies of my check-transmittal letters (20 March); I hope these well-calculated letters help smooth things over. Please make certain, personally, that those waivers come back to you duly signed.

Additional thought: contact your counterpart at the insurance office by telephone and confirm that they are <u>under no circumstances</u> to contact the next-of-kin. Their contract is with AH & S. The amounts we paid out are solely my executive decision. I think our settlements were fair and reasonable and in one case a little excessive, for as you know, Ed Blakey was on his way out. In other words, I want no post-payment awkwardness to cloud our future ADIF program. You handle it.

In conclusion, as we look down the road ahead, AH & S is now able to get stronger replacements for both Blakey and Gus Lyons, at a salary savings. Secondly, we cash-out an obsolete aircraft, and certain "inventories" aboard at the time while taking down a favorable cash balance of $85,000 on our little ADIF program. Finally, we can now re-think a new concept for all AH & S executive aircraft.

Well, it's late. I'm headed for the barn.

J. K. J.

MEMORANDUM

TO: A. K. Carver, Director of Operations (Aircraft)

Dear A. K.:

I am turning down your recent policy suggestion to schedule
AH & S aircraft for executive use only during daylight hours.

An airplane is no good on the ground. The cumulative
expenses of grounding both personnel and aircraft at nightfall
would be prohibitive. I am aware that some companies--not
our competition--follow the scheduling policies which you
ably suggest.

Al, I'm as sorry as you are about Gus's bad luck; I know
you flew with him a long time in the Fairchild. Nevertheless,
we have to rise above these things and carry on.

In this spirit, please forward at your earliest convenience
your recommendations for the acquisition of newer, possibly
more appropriate equipment to replace the Lockheed. You may
wish to recommend we step up to executive-jet aircraft.
Faster, more efficient aircraft would give us a needed edge
on our competition; but against this, most of our plants,
aside from Pennington and Mercer City, are in relatively
isolated areas all across the Eastern Seaboard. Are company
airstrips and/or nearby county facilities appropriate for
business jets?

A. K., I will read your realistic list/figures and recommendations
with considerable interest.

In closing, let me express a firm conviction: all AH & S
aircraft are extensions of the Executive/Sales thrust of
our Corporation. All aircraft and flying personnel must
hustle with the rest of us. Therefore, short-notice flights
at AH & S are routine. If we are not present first at the
Sales-Opportunity Point, then all of us might as well remain
grounded at the home office here in Pennington, Illinois.
Time is of the essence in modern marketing. It is a fact:
I ordered the Lodestar, crew, and passenger to report at
once to our newly acquired plant in West Virginia. I had to
do so on the evening of 5 March. I will do so again.

I expect your management of AH & S aircraft to implement the above goals each and every day.

Very cordially yours,

J. KELLY JOHNS
President and General Manager

Blind carbon copies:
- Maurice Cohen, Vice President, Finance
- Sheldon Thomas, Vice Presidnet, Personnel

ALLIED HIDE & SPECIALTY CO., INC.
1 TANNERY ROW
PENNINGTON, ILLINOIS

29 March 1972

Mr. Allen Oaker, Chairman-of-the-Board
Smyth-Oaker Investment Trust, Ltd.
505 Fifth Avenue
New York, New York

Dear Allen:

By now you have read the press accounts and have heard my
preliminary telephone report of the AH & S Lockheed "Lodestar"
accident not far from our newly acquired tannery at Healdsboro,
West Virginia, at about 20:00 hours, 5 March 1972. This is
a letter of clarification.

Regards the proximate cause of the accident, I confirm the
flight was duly authorized (Pennington to Healdsboro, direct)
and at this time the investigation is not conclusive. Two
facts must be stated: first, the Lockheed carried an Instrument Landing System, including glide path (and DEME); the
strip at Healdsboro had only a radio beacon. That tannery
being a recent acquisition, our flight crew was not entirely
familiar with the field. Secondly, in deteriorating weather
conditions, pilot error is indicated. They burned it approximately _five_ miles short of the runway.

I also lost Ed Blakey. Ed was a very gung-ho type. He
flew off on short notice to be in West Virginia for a morning
new-product (suede) conference. At the time I asked him if
a telephone call and forwarded suede samples would not suffice.
Ed wanted personally to see the new suede-run. So.

Regards follow-up action, I report the following:

a. The search for my new Manager of Sales (vice president)
   is underway. All of us out here wish to recruit outside
   AH & S: bring in new blood. If you have any personnel
   suggestions via your New York contacts, please advise.

b. My two pilots are being replaced.

c. Loss of the aircraft, added equipment, and certain
   inventory items are adequately covered by insurance.
   After routine survivor disbursements, our ADIF program
   brings in approximately $80,000.00.

d. Regards long-range planning, I see this unfortunate
   accident as an opportunity to upgrade my sales management
   and also to upgrade pilot personnel. Finally, I am now

103

in a position to take a hard look at the overall
efficiency of all our aircraft operations.

On the final point, I solicit your usual astute advice.
Your subsidiary is located in the middlewest; our present
tanneries and finish-plants are widely scattered. All-weather
aircraft operation is a necessity. What would you think of
going to jet equipment?

Beyond the above merely local issues, you will be pleased to
know your company has moved steadily ahead in the specialty-
leather field, with sales currently 8 percent ahead of last
year. The cost reduction program you ordered when I took over
out here is now paying dividends. I anticipate an even greater
share of the market in the next eighteen months.

As to Company-Community relations, the turnout for Blakey's
funeral tells us his talent for community relations was both
timely and has served its purpose. Doubtless he created the
new AH & S "image" in this small town. At last the old-line,
family ownership of this business is now virtually forgotten.

The "new" AH & S being a fact, I look forward to more fruit-
ful company-community relationships, a genuine Partnership for
Progress.

On a personal note, I find small-town life a little stulti-
fying, as does my wife Lou. Still there are small-town rewards,
most notably the close, lasting ties which one inevitably builds.
And, as always, there is an interesting job to do.

Faithfully,

J. KELLY JOHNS
President, and General Manager

104

Smith-Oaker Investment Trust, Ltd.
505 Fifth Avenue
New York, New York

Dear Johns:

Off to Bermuda for ten days work/vacation with British interests. Nevertheless, want to answer your recent report of 29 March (about your aircraft accident).

You state my company lost one twin-engined airplane, two pilots, one Sales Manager, plus some "inventory" and still made money. I don't know how you did it, and I don't care. Don't try to bootleg the $80,000.00 into your underline operating profits.

By inference you have repeatedly complained about Mr. Ed Blakey, but because Pennington is a small town, you lacked the guts to fire him. So you got a break: go out and find yourself a better man. I have no New York suggestions for a middlewestern based vice president of sales—in leather, or anything else.

Whether you upgrade your executive fleet of airplanes or not is entirely your decision. If a jet will make money, buy it; if it eats you up later, that's tough. Don't ask for a dime of financing from this end. I'd say exactly the same thing to any of my companies.

I remember Gus Lyons. A couple of times he flew me from Teeterboro out to Pennington. Very white hair, and chewed unlighted cigars. I thought he added a note of down-home cussedness to the whole proceedings. Sorry you lost him.

You state my subsidiary AH & S is making money. That's why I moved in on that down-at-the haunch, family-run picnic in the first place. That's exactly why I hired you to run it. For your future health and welfare I suggest you continue same. Your expenses are still out of line in comparison to industry-wide practice.

If you don't like Pennington, Illinois, say so. I can always find someone else who either does, or will lie to me about it.

I've got to leave.

Thanks for the info.

J. A. Oaker

J. Oaker

```
                              At Home
                              2223 Country View Terrace
                              Pennington, Illinois
                              5 April 1972

Mr. J. Kelly Johns, President
ALLIED HIDE AND SPECIALTY COMPANY, INC.
1 Tannery Row
Pennington, Illinois

Dear Kelly,
```

Only a month ago this evening, I got the terrible telephone call from our local radio station, wanting to know did I have any information about the airplane crash in West Virginia. It was Ed and poor Gus, and Bob Shambrough. Now I am pretty much "at home"; the neighbors have just been wonderful. The boys are fine.

I write to thank you for your thoughtfulness about the three checks. You are generous to pay the full monthly salary; the $15,000.00 really was totally unexpected. Edward never mentioned such a program to me, so I doubt if he, himself, knew about it. The "bonus" of $4,000.00 for the education of our two sons is a splendid suggestion. I have signed the checks (and the waivers) and have opened a bank account in the name of our sons. When they are older, you may rest assured I shall tell them the name of their benefactor. Our heartfelt gratitude.

Looking back on it, I also feel the funeral services were exactly as Edward might have wished. The cards and condolences from all who knew him--including all of his Little Leaguers-- are testimony of the high esteem in which he was held not only by the community of Pennington but also by his wonderful sales organization and their wives.

Surely Edward was a kind, generous man. The future was all before him.

I appreciate your willingness to be of further help. I will come past your office a little later this spring to "talk things over," when my future plans are more settled.

Again, thank you for all you have done for us.

```
                         Sincerely yours,

                         Barbara Blakey
                         (Mrs.) Barbara Blakey
```

R. F. D. Box 113
Millburgh, Illinois
7 April 1972 (a Friday)

Dear Mr. Kelly Johns,

Rec'vd the two checks. They are cashed. Thanks a lot.

You weren't the only one that missed Gus's funeral. Since they buried the Big Man in town at the same time, most of the Company people went to his if at all. Except for the hangar bunch. They came out here. Everybody. Maybe you like a closed-casket funeral, but I do not. Now I'll always have to remember Gus the way he was when he was called out on short notice that afternoon.

Which brings me to some points I want to make. I notice you ordered Gus paid from the first to the 14th (normal two-weeks pay); a big outfit like AH & S could have paid the whole month. But as Gus said, "Why, naturally they skin everything." That's what happened all right.

I signed your insurance check on the back not having much other choice. But I know and Gus knew it wasn't absolutely necessary to take off at five p.m. for a someplace in West Virginia he'd only been to once before and that one time in broad daylight. But you would have them go so they went. Gus called me at home from the telephone in the hangar and said, "Don't hold your breath on this one. Don't know when we'll get back." Well, that's what he was paid for, I guess.

And I will say this. The newspapers always claim a "pilot error." I will always think this one was caused by that high-time, righthand engine. If they was at altitude, in the overcast, and say the blower went out, was there anyplace else to come down except on a mountain? Maybe Gus wasn't the best on instrument flight, but I never did know him to be off any five miles on an approach. Gus knew the whole U.S., and it's not like him to be lower than any mountain, unless he knew for sure.

Well, what's past is past. If Gus had his choice he would always have flown during daylight hours as he observed you pretty much manage to do yourself.

Well thanks for the two checks and I've said in writing what's on my mind. And my name is not Mary, it's Maxine, and always was.

Yours truly,

Maxine Lyons

(Mrs.) Maxine Lyons

107

ALLIED HIDE & SPECIALTY CO., INC.
1 TANNERY ROW
PENNINGTON, ILLINOIS

8 April 1972

(Mrs.) Gustave Lyons
R. F. D. Box 113
Millburgh, Illinois

Dear Maxine Lyons:

I received your letter of 7 April and advise since you have signed and cashed the settlement checks, Mr. Lyon's salary account and his connection with the above-named company is terminated.

I have read carefully your thoughts on the possible causes of that tragic accident which saddened company personnel and the Pennington community. Nothing in the FAA or our own Company accident investigation reports substantiates your opinions.

Very truly yours,

J. KELLY JOHNS
President, and General Manager

My Work in California

The Younger Factory

Of the one hundred passengers arriving from Seattle (Boeing) my job was only with thirty-four industrialists from Asia. Of this group a dozen were unexpectedly tall; a few wore dark, prescription glasses; only one man had two briefcases as carry-on. Not one delegate looked back at the aircraft or took a picture of the Oakland charter terminal.

My welcome sign at the baggage claim area read in Japanese and Hindi: Industry Tour Delegates Here. They manufactured something or were of engineering backgrounds; therefore they were urbane and kept my placard in view but did not cluster about. Most of them spoke Oriental languages, but to me they used English: "Our weather is identical of here weather." "We have eaten considerately while at flying," and so on.

At the luggage carousel one man from Korea claimed only a backpack and a pair of blue skis. By way of explanation their chief delegate, a Mr. Hognisko, said our gentleman from Korea join this California Inspection at last minute: all very good.

Beyond the terminal entrance our bus was parked, its engine running.

For this I was relieved. In my work a great many things can go wrong.

Finally, our bus headed south towards San Leandro and the plant which was not far beyond Fremont.

By courtesy, Mr. Hognisko had boarded first and had claimed a seat immediately behind the driver. Now Mr. Hognisko leaned forward very intently; in a small notebook he recorded the RPM and fuel gauge readings. I made a mental note to arrange later for him actually to drive our bus—under supervision—inside the factory yard: a little thing like that for a delegate is very memorable.

As the bus went steadily through the last of the morning fog, I walked the aisle and answered their polite queries: Those salt flats at the edge of Upper Bay, were in production? The Alameda container-shipping facility, was it eighty-percent automated? Concerning Blacks in major California cities: how much Blacks?

The Korean's backpack was in the aisle beside him. Intensely, mostly with his arms, he was speaking to a man across the aisle; the man listened, did not change expression, but finally repeated the question to me in English:

"Gentleman with valuable pack here say he makes fashion-purses —very many. Also: how far is Disneyland?"

I replied that Disneyland was in the Los Angeles area, specifically at Anaheim, which was approximately four hundred miles south, about one hour flying time.

"Gentleman says Disneyland not so far away."

At first the factory appears on the horizon as several hundred aligned ventilators, exhaust stacks, and air-scrub towers; closer, the immense roofs rise slowly from the ground and fill the bus windows. Only then do they really see the factory walls.

I understand the reaction: they have flown a long way to see this absolutely state-of-the-art complex; in their own countries they may wish to build a replica. When at last in a moment of bus-window vision our factory becomes manifest, they fall silent, are a little reverent, a little stunned. I, myself, often view it at mid-morning in the California sunshine and still I have some slight feeling of awe.

Our bus stopped at the entrance gate: There will be a slight delay.

Actually, I believe these foreign-delegation delays have internal function. Not every unit of our Younger factory operates at any given time; therefore all tour routes are selectively programmed.

The question is a good one: as an experienced guide, have I seen the complete layout, all units in production? Or: have I ever been programmed twice on the identical tour-route? Possibly, but my sole interest is professional: the art of tour-satisfaction.

In about twenty minutes, as expected, a young woman in her three-wheeled golf cart rides out across the vast parking lot to our bus. She hands me the route-skip chart. Often we work together.

Inside our bus, the young woman from Public Relations speaks to this delegation in English, German, and then in Turkish. First, an apology for this routine delay. Then her rundown of statistics: number of fenced areas, square-footages under roof, water gallonage daily: the architects and major contractors for the Beginning, Middle, and Final Coordinate modules.

Her speech is always impressive. No questions.

As our delegation enters routinely through the East-Arch plaza, I sense the usual change of mood: casual talk ceases. Here the corridors are vaulted-steel, air-conditioned, and are virtually aseptic. The big surprise is the color-coding systems: all Receiving and Primary Incalculation areas are in tones of red; at tour's end, near the West Exit gates, the color coding ranges from indigo through violet.

Therefore, when this delegation looked down from a catwalk into their first full-production module, they saw that the nitrous tubing, conduits, and the work-persons' smocks were an identical shade of green. Because the high-speed machines are virtually silent, my voice was easily heard.

"Below, Gentlemen, our syntax looms. From left to right, inside translucent tubes, the Youngers are admitted, then loomed."

Each delegate at once became fascinated with a single aspect of the process: with the emission tubes or water-recovery sumps; with the sensor areas or the green, intricate thread-lines which glisten in the cool light. As though they were encased, merely passive objects, all Youngers are sorted, then pass at high speed through the looms. Here all syntax patterns were confirmed. No one person can ever register all the coordinated movements; in the end, all visitors merely stare.

"All loom thread is 90% nylon—linen is no longer used." And to Mr. Hognisko, "Syntax is a general term: in addition to speech, it also encompasses larger cultural patterns."

He made a note.

In the loom pits below, the machinery seemed to breathe, and for an instant to glow deeply inside the intricate thread barriers. A workperson, a woman in a green smock, emerged from the corridor between the extraordinary, winking shuttles, as though ejected or born from the loom itself; she glanced upward, gestured, then placed one hand lightly—testing for heat—on a rotor housing. The breathing looms slowed perceptively. The vault darkened as we moved on.

No further questions.

Our delegation lined up behind the glass barriers of a typical organic unit: here all Youngers receive their viral program injections; these modules are typical of one of the more advanced procedures.

All in a row, faces pressed to the glass barriers, the delegates watched intently. Smiling or asleep in their little sacs, the Youngers passing in the troughs seem almost a blur. When twins with Oriental features went past, the delegates gesticulated, were much pleased.

As we watched, the sensor banks read the fluid codes: abruptly, the twins were shunted off together, disappeared. Farther along we viewed the more refined sorting and incalculation: one strain was for sensitivity to metal objects (cards, gold coin, tempered steel— as in guns). This one is standard, takes very well. The more complex motives of power (money and banking) or indiscriminate knowledge (for teachers) is less predictable.

From my point of view, however, nothing *seems* to happen in the organic modules; they are low delegate interest. The crux forge and the sports verifier are more melodramatic. For Youngers, however, the entire process is without pain; doubtless it passes in a mild semi-biotic dream. As to overall effectiveness, not all types of irradiated tendencies are final; in California, a complete program-rejection at some later age is not common. Being exotic, our viral incalculation modules elicit few questions.

None? Very well: move along now to a typical production unit, V.T.

In V.T. all action is overt. Here all delegates have floor privilege. They may stand at a machine-of-choice. They move about freely. Only a repeated call for the lunch-snack disengages most foreign observers. I also like these sections quite a bit.

Of course, the unexpected noise is the first contrast. The hubbub is most life-like: here all the machine operators call out. They curse one another and their balky machines; they chew tobacco where they stand. In V.T. the work rules are posted in several languages, especially Spanish; the operators belong to a loose, ineffectual union. Here Management leaves well enough alone.

At once all delegates scattered. Now they stood beside the machines, avidly speaking with the operators, if only in sign language. At last here was something everyone understood.

Mr. Hognisko was immediately beside a Stealth Elaborator. The Younger is placed (in sac) on a rotating metal plate; the eccentrically-balanced flywheel lowers—delicately or too deeply—and roughs the sac with the wheel's random abrasives. All Youngers appear to be terribly shocked, are in momentary pain; inside the sac we see their little hands row the fluid. Oddly, however, certain Youngers laugh; others withdraw or become merely fetal. The fascination, of course, is with the *variety* for at the Violence Tannery no two Youngers ever react precisely in the same way. The reason for this is not known.

No matter: because of altercations and workmen shouting obscenities, there can be neither questions or answers. Naturally these conditions divert delegates from our more refined techniques: A & A (Animal Affiliation, usually of the horse-prone variety); A & T (Alliance and Trauma-consequence, as in multiple divorce); A & C (Attenuated Cruelty, wide-spectrum). If asked directly, I say those more isolated sheds are reserved for some future visitation.

Because this particular delegation would not leave the machines, time did not permit them a view of the flower-decked, elaborately color-coded Reunion Ramps. Here all Youngers are delivered— emotionally, melodramatically—to parents, guardians, etc. With manufacturers, a little reconciliation doubtless goes a long way, for their interest is with distribution. In any event, after our luncheon-snack I answered questions:

—Yes: all water is re-cycled. Our California model conforms to Regional and Federal clean-air standards, or is being modified accordingly.

—No: Those Upper-Bay salt flats have no bearing on this choice of site.

In some distant area of the plant, at a place I have never been, I heard a reverberating, deep, explosion. All cafeteria lights went dim—then again became bright.

The delegates looked at each other but did not change expression.

Through a third party who spoke some English, the man from Korea asked about profit margins, and projected return on capital investment.

These figures, I said, are not available at the present time.

Before lunch was over, I noted that Mr. Hognisko has disappeared.

When we went outside to our boarding ramp, I saw Mr. Hognisko driving our bus (under supervision). He steered in large, swerving figure-eights, all over the now totally deserted parking lot.

When the regular bus driver saw me waiting, he directed Mr.

Hognisko to park at our ramp.

As they boarded, each delegate said the tour had been most interesting and educational.

Whereupon I returned with the delegation to a downtown San Francisco hotel and checked them in for the night.

II. *The Snow Orchestration*

A Bedouin party had toured California sixteen days when I was detailed to their "caravan" at a highway intersection just south of Yosemite.

Majestically, their polished-aluminium motor coaches all in a row floated around a curve, became larger; closer, in the mid-morning sun, the silver coaches seemed still wet. They parked in echelons-of-two beside the highway. Beneath the windshields, I saw sprayed-on, national colors; all license plates were of diplomatic issues. Their coaches carried twenty-eight persons, excluding drivers; the TV, radio, citizen's band antennae, and the rooftop air conditioners implied money was no object. They were much more than one hour late.

When no one got out, I walked from my car back to the first motor coach. Above and from behind his windshield, a driver in white coveralls waved casually. Their door did not open until I knocked again.

The Sheik greeted me cordially. He was in native dress and spoke with a distinct Cambridge accent. We shook hands. Inside it was a series of elaborate, meaningless introductions in Arabic; I presumed the names and titles were also on my roster.

The large forward compartment of this coach was lined with satin pillows; a white canopy of cloth hung overhead. With water-pipes and provocative sex magazines scattered about, the effect was that of a lavish tent, temporarily at ease on a desert oasis. From each dais, however, I noted each Arab could see both the driver's back and the instrument panel of the coach.

Naturally, my concern was to discuss at once our exercise: its engineering, cultural function, project costs, and projected useful life—everything. Unfortunately, either it was now tea time or I was served ritualistically. Inwardly I fretted at this further dalay but made conversation and watched them drop many lumps of sugar into their delicate teacups. Time passed. The canopy filled with blue, sweet, Arabic smoke.

Suddenly an older man who had remained withdrawn in shadows leaned forward. He spoke emotionally in Arabic. I understood not a word, but I felt accused—of something.

"This cousin," the Sheik said not calmly, "*believes* one of our drivers is a State Highway Patrolman. In disguise, of course."

I requested details.

"As we go, we hear only this driver: *his* citizen-band radio is *active*. On our monitor in this coach we hear his *every* word."

They nodded: it was a communal judgment.

"This Number-Three driver conveys—Oh, slyly in code—information."

Patiently, I explained: all caravan drivers assigned are Teamster-Union members. By custom these drivers, via CB, convey harmless greetings to other passing Teamster-Union drivers. They alert one another to speed traps, the presence of Highway Patrol cars, and so on.

"But we have diplomatic plates!"

Finally I resolved it by two promises: a possible substitute driver; secondly, immediate warning to Number Three. Meanwhile, with their permission, I would brief all drivers; on this final leg to the valley ahead their caravan would simply follow my official car. This was discussed at some length: agreed.

Therefore I walked back to the other coaches to alert the drivers and to counsel Number Three—who appeared to be Pakistani. The third and fourth coaches carried only women and children. On identical television consoles I saw the identical program, an episode from "Gunsmoke"—with Arabic soundtrack. The women in *perda* and their children watched the screens very intently.

Number-Five coach carried servants, supplies, one accountant-scribe, and a physician; inside it smelled rancid with coffee grounds, smoke, and household pets.

At the head of the convoy, from the middle of the highway, I waved one arm in a circle: start your engines.

Slowly I led the way upward along the treacherous, curved highway for another sixty-two miles. We were now so behind schedule that the two guards at the gateway arch of stone waved us immediately to the promontory. Not far from the guard rails at the cliff's edge, the motor coaches again parked in echelons-of-two. Again I walked back to their first coach and knocked several times to gain admission.

I said the news was good: although well past noon, the atmospheric conditions at the altitude were still satisfactory. Our observation parapets lay immediately ahead.

Most opportunely, the Sheik said, this pause coincides precisely with the customary hours for lunch. Naturally I would be their honored guest?

"Very well," I had to reply, for clearly my status was that of servant. "Possibly this pause is foreordained—for our better fellowship?"

Everyone who understood smiled; my remark was then translated. The older men nodded wisely, then repeated in Arabic what I thought was the word "foreordained."

Our meal was elaborate. The lamb and the goat had been slaughtered, then fast-frozen in their home country, flown to California, and only last night delivered by taxi to this caravan. I admired the planning; the Sheik replied that such was their custom while abroad. Eventually everyone took a waterpipe and began to smoke. More time passed.

Almost inadvertently, much later, I glanced at my wristwatch.

Everyone stood up as though I, myself, had engendered this by-now-ruinous delay. At once two men took citizen-band microphones from beneath their pillows and began to give orders. Then everyone was talking at once in Arabic.

When all members of the party gathered on the promontory, there was a drawn-out uninformed discussion: was the snow exercise suitable for male children (under puberty), women, or servants? Eventually the physician, all young girls, and the eldest women were returned to the caravan; for security, all drivers to remain *in* their vehicles—and no CB transmissions.

So it was very late when finally I led their party to the viewing ramparts. Once seated, the Bedouins wrapped themselves in their robes and stared at the amphitheater headwalls of granite. Already I saw shadows in the east crevasse.

Over an intercom which connects all observation sites, I gave the set-speech: superb feat of modern technology superbly adapted to the unusual California resources and terrain. The exercise exploits three basic elements: light, wind-activation, and snow. Although apparently preserved in its superb natural state, our amphitheater below in fact is artfully lined with recessed ducting, elaborate banks of discharge nozzles, and panels of sequestered lights. From geothermal wells—Nature's bounty—high-density CO_2 rises, is compressed, and is then released sequentially. The gas escaping becomes "snow." All energy-transfer systems draw power from distant hydroelectric sites. Hurriedly, I reviewed the volume of released gasses, miles of buried tubing, square-footage estimates, the main designers, primary contractors, and maintenance budgets, *per capita*. Were there questions?

If the Bedouins registered my voice, they gave no sign.

Oddly—I confess it—when an orchestration begins, I forget the parties visiting. No two orchestrations are identical; I am always surprised. In one way I am proud to be part of it, and at those moments I wish everyone in the world could share this experience, especially when the program is complete and in sunlight at noon—which is the proper time.

As always, and especially with the Bedouin party, I had the usual feeling of anticipation—something like terror—when the first flakes of snow floated upward from the walls. Lights suddenly transformed the vast granite amphitheater into alabaster. The first "winds" blew. The panoramic wall began imperceptibly to writhe.

The snow builds, is caught in random drifts as though the wind were a shaping hand: the first portraits emerge. As it is with the vast faces carved in stone against the sky at Mount Rushmore, so now do portraits of snow range across the light-breathing walls for our initial contemplation. Because of the programmed wind, the hair on the snow-sculptured heads seems to rise as though the massive heads had tossed back in pain from the azure light.

On this particular day the faces at once extended into full-length figures: two prehistoric Asiatics in postures of sacrifice, their ritualistic knife piercing again and again the maimed child of snow. Face averted, an Indian woman undulates in postures of sexual invitation below the priest who is riding a burro. Whereupon the amphitheater resolves into concentric rings, each ring smaller and lower until the lowest depths become an eye, an enfolded flower of blazing snow, more fluid, more gold than the sun at noon. From the top rings, driven by winds, the snow overflows then falls like giant slabs of wax dripping into the molten eye. Always I imagine music would contribute to their better understanding of our past, but there is no sound beneath the sky.

The full-length figures dissolve into violet light. Now there is a

117

wall of forests, all trees falling. Oxen and a thousand horses rear or are solidly yoked, pulling first crude sledges across the headwall, and then pulling grotesque mills down, down through a crevasse into that deepest core. All growing things are now gone away, the walls turn incredibly green, are supine beneath the faceless wind. These things I know are prelude only and I wait.

The sun came to rest on the farthest rim of the mountain. That first suggestion of nightfall was like the giant, whistling shadow of a bird's wing scything above our parapets.

The snow orchestration became suddenly frenzied. The lights blinked, shuddered; the wind rose. Everywhere snow erupted, became untrammeled drifts, then rolled down, down, as a thousand small avalanches into the darkness.

The amphitheater became mauve, then red. The wind swirled, lifted the red snow in rising, cyclonic columns. At eye-level those columns tilted, and I saw into the calyx of a monstrous flower. Within, I saw neither face nor figure—only the snows: iridescent, without motion, a roil of fire wherein nothing burned.

The lights turned a violent orange. The snow column died into the fissures of the granite wall; the wind also went away. As though the world itself had ended, there was neither breath nor sound.

In that spectacular, truncated way—abruptly—the orchestration of snows for the Bedouins stopped. If viewed in sunlight at noon, they would have understood everything; they, themselves, had delayed. I made no apology. I did not explain.

Their robes blown by late-evening winds, the Bedouins straggled back in little groups to the darkening promontory and to their aligned coaches. Only the guardrails seemed unchanged.

As it turned out, however, I never did answer the usual questions. At once their physician and their accountant-scribe requested audience.

Very mysteriously, Number-Three driver had disappeared. He had transmitted no CB messages; no property was missing; no known enemies. With the Sheik, I inspected that coach; the driver had simply vanished.

At once the Sheik withdrew with his immediate family and counselors. I waited outside the closed vehicles for what seemed a very long time. Finally, everyone reappeared and I was told a decision:

Most assuredly this thing was unfortunate. On the other hand, could it be entirely astonishing: had not I, myself, agreed previously both to reprimand and also to driver-replacement? Being a Pakistani—very possibly naturalized for convenience—the man was obviously incompetent. For this surely the Teamsters Union bears much blame. Concerning the driver's family: in any way, here or abroad, might they be contacted?

I said probably in some way they could be tracked down.

Excellent. But to the main point: an alternate driver.

I did not reply.

"Being the most qualified," the Sheik said, "by reason of my own extensive limousine holdings, *I* will drive this vehicle for the remainder of this day. I have closely observed all drivers—also the instrument panel. For me this will be educational. Agreed?"

I said the next stop was outside Fresno, where they were expected.

"Well done," the Sheik said very affably, for he was eager to drive.

One-by-one the engines started. Their noise reverberated upward in the chilled, rising wind from the mountains.

Going back down the highway, the Sheik followed my automobile much, much too closely. Continually he honked the airhorns. He drove recklessly—on the inside of all curves.

At that time—and to this day—it was pointless for me to report to anyone higher up that very plainly I saw bloodstains near the driver's seat when I inspected the vehicle. I suspected their physician. But as the Sheik had so rightly said, "We have diplomatic plates."

No matter: at the final intersection their caravan turned south. I honked once, and waved goodbye. In my report I intended to say that—in fact—the delegates noted many parallels between our snow orchestrations and their own rich, essentially Persian cultural heritage.

Exactly at the speed limit I drove north to my motel which was at the edge of Stockton.

III. *At the Coma Pavilions*

"My hobby geology," the surveyor from Penang told me. "Long time ago this place under water."

I said probably so.

On our drive south to the coast this group of scholars, a recuperating Swiss physician, educators, etc., had become better acquainted and were now a lively, well-motivated interest group. Our station wagons were to park here; older ladies—probably ex-schoolteachers —changed to hiking boots for this last-mile descent to the valley floor.

No recording equipment or cameras beyond this point, please.

Below, melodramatically, the valley divides; each parallel branch ends in white sand at the beach. Beyond, the sea was iridescent, rising, turquoise. For me this tour marked the season's end; already I was thinking of Palm Springs.

Energetically, our ex-schoolteachers started down the path; farther along, one voice, in German, began a marching song. Mainly to permit the Swiss physician a moment's rest beneath the rock overhang of a shelter carved years ago from solid rock by the first inhabitants, I called a halt and then reviewed our inspection guidelines:

Speech with inhabitants permitted *only* if resident-initiated. However: technically qualified observers—physicians, our pathologist, etc.—may touch or otherwise manipulate comatose subjects. Only gross anatomical evaluations are customary; use of a stethoscope is all right. "Why-type" queries are unsettling, hence counterproductive. In a word, ladies and gentlemen, we are professionally-oriented observers.

"Yes, yes," the group responded, mostly in English. "Is understood."

Questions?

—Certainly: All of them enjoy State, Federal, and Constitutional safeguards regardless of race, etc. Percentage of resident, native Californians is not available—estimates vary, yes.

—No: not an "exhibit" or a "theme park" impulse (e.g., Under Six Flags). If motivations appear incomprehensibly complex, consider the complexity of life today.

No others? I thank you.

Around the first, abrupt corner, against the sky and almost bridging the canyon walls, they saw their first Counseling Mobile. The light was very good.

To me, this one is largely amusing. To all educators and to our shockingly emaciated priest, *en route* to the Vatican, it was fascinating. At once, they climbed the ladders and from the high platforms leaned over the railings the better to observe.

I explained the site-logic: here coastal winds converge where the canyon narrows. The boom and cable arrangements suspended also converge—then regress—from the Resource Wheel—the large one, centered horizontally. The dissonant noises are their voices and also wind among their cables. In mid-air, the subjects forever pass; being electrically charged, however, they can never touch. By attraction, then repulsion they move continually—what, one hundred fifty feet above these rocks?

Suddenly, exhibitionistically, one in a loincloth, its body dried totally by the winds, swooped down: arms outstretched, wide-eyed, the sun caught as fire on its enormous, steel-rimmed glasses. For a second it was suspended above our astonished heads, then with tackle screaming, it rose in a great rush of air, was gone.

"Dead," the Swiss physician said. "Long time." Our pathologist from Edinburgh, concurred.

Aloft on the highest platforms the educators tried to interpret the sound of the cables and the voices in the sibilant air. Again I called: Rejoin, please your group immediately?

Because the sun was not yet too high we walked mostly in the shade of the canyon walls. Being of mature years, this group viewed with little interest the Excess Pavilions: a Consumer Cavern, the Cervix-Renewal and Depletion Station where desires of a purely sexual nature are changed monthly by surgical intervention. Surprisingly, the emaciated priest scarcely paused at an elaborate Meditation Pavilion dedicated to programmed Faith-Loss.

Their age-group considered, possibly I kept them overly long at the Matriarch Escarpment. I, myself, am oddly drawn to this ever-expanding sequence which is best viewed from elevated walkways along the opposite canyon wall. I explained:

Opposite: a typical encampment painted ochre and blue. Architecturally, the primitive forms hang on: seen in the platforms, square or shaped to the cliff face; observed in the child-transfer poles (one per sibling) anchored like horizontal flagpoles, extending out from the platforms; also below—bars vertical or horizontal—their individual men-pens. Now: either supine or pacing continually in the prescribed patterns—two examples visible, extreme left—the woman controls all architectural improvements, equipage, monies. Moreover . . . .

"A-hoh!" the priest said, for he was coughing. Deeply absorbed, the Swiss physician said nothing, but his nurse spoke vehemently, "Disgusting, I think." The physician nodded, "Is so."

Along the cliffs, the women had finished eating and had fed the

121

little children—gentle or with cruel dispatch. Actually, I find the children very pleasing to watch, for they frolic about the platforms, at times terrifyingly near the unguarded edge. Now, however, it was time for them to descend.

Note the psychological play. Having been fed, the children understand they are to be lowered, head-down, from the anchored flagpoles to the man-cage level of the structure. While being rigged by the ankles for their over-the-canyon suspension, the children whimper or kick. If a reactive type, the mother screams; if brutal, she often abuses the child.

Observe: at the instant of lowering, a child now smiles, laughs, calls to the man! See the Black babies bounce and whirl themselves and sing out?

At cage-level, the man reaches out. Variously he speaks, touches the girls' genitals, see? Swings them far out over the canyon—their play. Soon the man gives each suspended child its ritualistic midday bath. So: now along the escarpment, high and low, the children are raised back to the mother's platform. Now their little faces are very sober, or they simulate tears, or great glee—as the mother requires. There: all done for this day.

Being myself the son of parents long separated, a Pomona College graduate, and as a person who lives in celibacy—save the two winter months at Palm Springs—really, I am drawn to this escarpment. In fact, I forgot to ask for questions.

The surveyor from Penang spoke. "How make more babies?"

"At night," I replied. "Someway at night."

"Surely," the pathologist said, "there is a hole in the platforms. Possibly by a trapdoor access is gained—after dark or not."

"Hole somewhere," the surveyor replied. "But why he go up there anymore?"

A discussion ensued and eventually I led this group to the place where first we hear plainly the long, cloth-tearing sound of waves dying on the white sands.

Among thwarted beach pine and oak trees at the valley's mouth, in pits, or aloft on poles exposed to the heavy sledge of the sun, abruptly, we came upon crucifixion platforms.

The stench of kelp and ruined shellfish at first is shocking, but this group did not at all draw back from this littoral of self-imposed agonies. The pathologist and the surveyor and the German philologist (ret.) ran forward to see more. In a second all the others scattered wildly among the trees.

Abandoned, I watched them go. Officially, I appear interested in a great many things; unofficially, however, my enthusiasms cannot be totally legislated from higher up. In my work-year of ten months, I see no other place of such consummate, natural beauty; yet, inwardly, I find this quarter-mile of sand truly revolting. Farther along I hear even the ex-schoolteachers cry out among the oak trees at some macabre, almost-sought-for recognition. In this place I keep my personal participation to the level of description, and the tight little smile.

In general: our Crucifixion Beach presents three general categories: Situations-Financial (Credit Pits, Tax-Supplicators, and others); Conformist Poles (Stakes, also Bamboo); and finally, the Coma-Pavilions proper. Since no one in the party either wanted or needed to hear more, I went directly ahead to the place where they would re-assemble. As I walked rapidly ahead, certain members of our party called out.

Two school teachers, their walking boots deep in sand, asked about a woman, burned by the sun, her hair blowing, seated—or buried—navel-deep in her pit. Mechanically, steadily, the woman threw sand upward into the wind; the wind blew the sand back into the pit and into her eyes. "Either credit-possessive," I explained, "*Or* a person forever sailing on packaged tours. It is the same. By going deeper she expects—some-time—to find water, from the sea."

The Swiss doctor was separated from his nurse. He was beside a platform about the height of a hospital bed, the platform larger than a circus ring, made up of old hatch covers, planks, and other flotsam from the sea. The bodies—perhaps one hundred—were hopelessly intertwined, comatose, save for the eyes which at random opened, stared for awhile at the sun, then closed. Stethoscope in place, the doctor was tracing the arterial blood supplies in the arms and the legs of the men and women. On his right hand the doctor wore a rubber, surgical glove. He glanced up from his very serious examination and said, "Nefer hemerrhoids in a homosexual—I have nefer seen it."

The professional educators and also the German philologist (ret.) called down from the very top of a conformist pole. Aloft those poles sway in the wind, first towards the valley of stone, then towards the sea. their voices seemed to be calling, "Accounted for

. . . allll accounted for . . . ." but I could not be certain.

Even the priest, who was said to be *en route* to the Vatican and who had heard so much during his life, was apparently overwhelmed. Withdrawn in shadows, I passed him beside the pilings of some vast towering platform. In sand, from below, he stared aloft at the underpinnings. The priest was extraordinarily pale beside the black, creosoted poles.

The surveyor from Penang was the first to join me as I waited at the exit path where pines and oak and sand almost touch the tides running.

Without wishing to be so, I was sitting eye-level before the final and certainly the largest single pavilion. Here incredibly old men and women sit on a platform, elaborately put together, iron-reinforced against any storm. In the wind, in the terrible sun, at night and in salt spray these persons beyond speech each hour thrust thorns, or splinters of wood, or even fractured abalone shells —any debris—beneath their own flesh, and into the shoulders and the backs of one another.

In the end, always, their infections are overwhelming and they lie down, more than a thousand, still working, still moving a little, then comatose, unable to register either the sea or clouds, the valley or the sun burning in the sky overhead. Forever, their large and their small wounds fester, suppurate, fester, and grow.

"Okay," the surveyor said after awhile. "They pay for something?"

I said probably so.

Only when the first shadows rose from the sea and fell all at once across the beach did this party leave the Pavilions and gather at the exit path. Going back, no one at all sang. This day and this season were now ending. For the first time since I began this kind of employment, I found it a little depressing: for the past hour I had waited, and had thought vividly of Palm Springs. The station wagons were still parked on the cliff above.

Only after we were on the freeway returning to the hotels and to the city from whence we had come did the surveyor from Penang whisper in my ear:

"German, one who start singing. He stay back there. On a pole."

I did not reply. The pathologist and the priest and the Swiss physician were already asleep, and besides these things happened more often than the surveyor knew: about two per party, on a yearly average.

The station wagon seemed to throw itself even faster through the dark, headed towards the high, lighted escarpment of the San Francisco skyline. I thought only about tomorrow—and of Palm Springs.

This year, again, no doubt I will meet someone interesting.

I always do.

Getting Married

I am not pretty, nor was I a very clever girl around boys. On the other hand, I am pleasant, and understanding, and was glad to find I could become very domestic—I mean loving—after I married Burney.

K.O. Burney: not Kenneth, or Karl, but only the initials. After he moved into my father's rental apartment above our garage, Burney once told me he had a brother somewhere in the Armed Forces whose name was O.K. (initials only). How could any mother ever, ever name her two sons K.O. and O.K.? From that remark I understood from the first that his family was not advantaged. I mean less advantaged than my own family.

My father has his own two-chair shop, and was once the Secretary-Treasurer of his fraternal order. Mother is somewhat less social, but she gets what she wants. Mother was working for her beautician's license when she married Daddy. I am the only child, the kind of girl that tried hard in high school but always got C + . After graduation—as our neighbors said—I was "at home."

"A-what?" was the exact word Burney said the first day I really spoke to him—and got an answer.

He had been in the garage apartment three months and had paid promptly in cash. Both mother and father thought he was steady, but I must say he kept his own counsel. He was just wiggling out from beneath his 1953 Ford coupe. He was three years older than me, the kind of man who has never thought himself attractive, for he had not helped his best feature. I mean, his hair. It was just a gorgeous, deep copper against the concrete, there in the sunlight.

"Thanks-no."

I had asked, did he want to lay under his car on our old chenille spread, the cement being no doubt very chilly. Yet the way he said

127

"Thanks-no" was neither rude nor common. He simply did not know exactly how to accept little neighborly things.

Logically, even ruthlessly, he began to wipe grease from his hands. He used one little ball of waste, then tossed it aside in a neat pile beside the back step where I sat watching him.

I said my name was Dora. He looked at me in a very manly way, daring me to flinch: "K.O. Burney, here."

Probably I looked vague, but I said, "How-do-you-do, *Mister* Burney." I certainly was not going to discuss his name, so I asked him about his car.

"Oh, I just want it *right*. I mean . . . ."

It seemed the car leaked oil from the gasket behind the water pump. He hated for something he owned free and clear to be dripping oil all over his half of the garage. "I want things right. That's all."

I thought our first conversation was over, but he surprised me. In the way of shy people—for no real reason—he became suddenly very talkative. I realized he was also a lonely man.

It seemed this particular Ford was not a bad old car. Got him to the Plant, and back. Liked to keep it tip-top, and that's why he owned his own tools. That way you got full value and you didn't have to trade every year for the benefit of Detroit . . . .

Burney nodded his head in a straight line from our back steps in Haskall—near Chicago—towards Lake Michigan, and towards Detroit, beyond. The way he said it, Detroit was a bad city.

"My father says that too,"—and I could have bit my tongue. Really, I wanted to agree with Burney because what he said seemed accurate; I did not want him to think I was playing up to his opinions.

"I doubt it," K.O. Burney said, and picked up all his balls of waste and put them in a little brown paper sack and put the sack in the Ford. You could tell he would throw that sack in a trash barrel at the first service station he saw. His gesture told me that the Glaspys—father *and* daughter—need not worry about trash left around by K.O. Burney.

Still, he had caught me in a little lie, and I felt he was right to do so: Daddy's new Plymouth was parked in our side of the garage. He did trade, every two years.

I changed the subject.

"Electronics," Burney said, and I understood he was more than a semi-skilled workman at Teletek, our new plant out beyond Sparkman. Even in high school he had realized electronics was an expanding field—so he got into it. And no regrets.

Burney worked at a bench inside, with meters and clips and wires, testing telemetry equipment. His hands were white with very long supple fingers. Even today he does not realize his long fingers are a great point of his beauty. It's not the sort of thing a new wife can say to someone like Burney—even after dark.

Abruptly, he walked once around the car. He sighted along the door panel—no dents or dings. He sighted back along our driveway towards the street. He got in the car and slammed the door.

"Got to take off," he said, and backed his car very fast all the way to the street. He did not even say goodbye.

That is how we met. I was certain he had no business elsewhere, except to throw away that little brown sack of waste. It was his afternoon off work; he probably drove around and around by himself until it was time to park somewhere and eat.

My mother was looking down at me from our kitchen window. Behind the pane of glass her lips were saying, "You come in here right now . . ."

That was a Saturday in spring, two weeks before I graduated from high school.

At first I had no feeling at all about K.O. Burney, except that he was interesting. He had unusual ideas—things he had worked out for himself.

More than once that spring, after he had washed his car on the ramp, we sat in the front seat in plain sight of the kitchen window, and talked. He told me the difference between AM and FM broadcasting, and how radar works, and about the power-pack and the detector stages of ordinary radio and TV sets. I really understood it. I just knew he could have been a wonderful teacher, especially science.

"What I don't like," he said once, "is the way everyone takes a piece of the working man. I *know* that."

Generally, I believed if a man worked and managed well, then he would get ahead.

"Don't believe what they show you on TV," he said, and smiled bitterly. "At war, or at a hanging, it's the working man first."

"Well, help yourself," I said. "You have a union. Don't they have powers?"

That was what my father said, who was never himself a union barber and who did not like to have a union man in the second chair.

"You really think so, Dora?" and Burney lowered his voice. He looked directly at me. "Union big shots are no different from Senators or Generals or Henry Ford in Detroit."

I had never thought that unions might also oppress a working man. Burney was not cynical or bitter, but he was the first person I ever met who knew from real experience how the world runs. And he had other good ideas.

"Those so-called services," and now he looked straight ahead through the clean windshield as though we were going down the road very fast. "Checking accounts. Time payments. Why, working people ought to buy for less. But we pay more, in interest. You figure it out sometime . . ."

"Dora," he said after a little while. "Some things ain't right."

"Aren't."

"Aren't," Burney said and to this day he has never said that other word in my presence.

For a long time nothing happened. I do not know exactly what I was thinking.

Then mother was on the ramp, and I rolled down the window. She was dressed, or at least as much dressed up as she ever gets to go out with father.

"Now *Dor-a* . . . ." *Oh, how I knew that tone.*

"Your father and me already had our snack but I didn't know you were out here. With Mr. Burney, I mean."

Mother smiled very sweetly and said, "Are you sitting for someone?"

Mother knew very well I did not have a baby-sitting job that evening.

"So, why don't you have Mr. Burney take you to 12th and Sparkman. That's the Drive-Inn."

I was so mortified, I could have cried.

"Here's a dollar. Get what you want."

I said nothing at all, but I could have struck her—or something. It was as though Burney wanted to run my errands, or as though he could not possibly have enough money for a Drive-Inn sandwich.

"Also. *We* will be home soon. It's Ladies' Auxiliary."

That was mother's way of saying, "You come straight home, young lady." After all, I was out of high school, even if I had no real job in mind.

But what hurt me most was the look on Burney's face: he had been told to do something unpleasant. Besides, he had never so much as asked me to go for a ride, much less to go on a date.

Nevertheless, Burney took us across town. What else could he do?

The car hop was a boy from my high school class. When he put his head half inside the car, his cheeks seemed to switch from red to white in the neon or the headlight beams of other parked automobiles. When the car hop heard what Burney said, he smirked.

"Now look, Mac," Burney said. The boy was startled. "I said two checks. Separate bills. Now you do that."

The car hop drew back, and suddenly seemed very thin, as though standing sideways in the outside light. "Yes *sir* . . ."

For the first time I heard Burney's voice of absolute command. I mean he had character. If the car hop had said another word, Burney would have gotten very slowly out of our car—and then I don't know what might have happened.

Actually, Burney did not show bad temper. He was very firm, and he was doing what he thought was the right thing: respecting my mother's wishes.

Oh, I should have made the best of it, too. I should have been more pleasant, but what I ate did not taste good. I could not think of a single thing to talk about. We sat there in silence.

Only after we were driving home, I looked at him sitting beside me.

"I—I guess it just proved you right, Burney."

"How so?"

"Taking advantage of the working man. I am sorry if I spoiled your night out."

"Look," he said, and parked in the front of our curb, but did not turn off the lights or the car motor.

"I'm doing all right. The way things are."

I understood from that only one thing: his job, the apartment, and his future in electronics were the main thing. If he were single-minded about the way he lived, I admired him for that.

"So forget it. Right?"

As I walked in front of his car, through his car lights, I held my head high.

Inside, I went directly to bed. I lay there for a long time and hated my mother. Finally I blamed myself. I should have been more pleasant, and should have made the most of it.

But if that is really what I thought, then why did I cry?

All that summer I was at loose ends. Mother and father would have sent me to beautician's school, but that seemed so common, so unrewarding. We talked about Polly Potter Secretary School, in the fall; in July I interviewed for the Telephone Company. At least we agreed on one thing: I did not want to be an airline hostess. I had no fear of flying, but I did not want to sleep each night in a strange hotel room. Being an only child, I did not want—secretly—to leave home. Not yet.

If Burney was on the night shift, I saw him arrive back at the apartment each day as we were eating breakfast. On collection days, to keep down unnecessary noise, I carried the trash cans farther away from his window. Or at night, if he was off-shift, we sat on the back steps. We talked about everything. He was a great deal more lonely than he, himself, realized. His father was killed in a bulldozer accident; then his mother lived in Topeka and Wichita and Independence, Missouri. One night he told me he had dropped out of high school to enlist in the Army for electronic school. Had Burney not told me, I never would have guessed.

In August Burney worked the day shift. He had no idea of stoves or cooking for himself—except from cans. Each Friday I gave his place a good cleaning, and that's what I was doing—his dishes—when I heard his car stop on the ramp below. I heard his feet walk up the stairs.

By the time Burney came in—and caught me—I had my hands dry. He stood in the door. I had a terrible electric feeling all over my skin. He was very white—pale.

"You're hurt!"

"Burney stepped inside. He held out his white, roller-bandaged hand for me to see.

"Bit me," and I realized he was shaken. I smelled the adhesive tape and burn ointment. "Two-twenty volts. When I jerked back, why a wire looped right around my hand and . . . ."

I had just remade his bed. I led him towards it, because he was so pale and weak from the shock. Burney was going to sit down on the edge of the bed, and that made him turn towards me.

I just couldn't help myself. When I saw his hurt, pale face something seemed to shatter inside me—like a blue bowl dropped on tile.

I threw my arms around him. I kissed him—just to comfort him. I held him to me and said, "Oh, poor baby . . . ."

That's all I said, and that was exactly the way I meant it. We must have stood there for only a moment—but oh, it was beautiful.

"What do *I see!*"

Mother was standing in his apartment door.

Burney sat down on the edge of his bed. Quickly he hid his bandaged hand behind his back—as though ashamed of his injury.

I never got a chance to explain. Mother was absolute. And terrible.

"I'll tell you what *I* see," she shouted.

She came into his apartment. She looked around, her eye vicious as a bird's. She lowered her voice.

"I *see* a trollop. Also a *man*—old enough *to know better.* I see two sneaks. And I see now what I should ought to have seen beneath my own eyes on my own property all along . . . . Well Sir?"

I wanted Burney to get up and slap her. But he did not. I wanted him to explain—the way I could not. I wanted anything but silence, and Burney staring at the floor. Perhaps he was in real pain, but he said nothing at all.

Burney held up his bandaged hand, but mother did not notice it. If Burney were pale, mother knew it was guilt, and fear of her.

"So we will just put a stop to this," she said. "You two will be married. Forthwith and notwithstanding. *And* Sunday's the day. And that's *that.*"

Burney slowly got up from the bed. He went to the door of the apartment. I thought he might walk right on out, and down the steps, and go away forever. In my heart I wished he would—almost.

With his head, he gestured to my mother: get out.

"No," he said to me when I began to follow her. "You stay here."

I did what Burney said.

For a while he walked up and down the apartment, his eyes on the floor.

"Now look here: were you in on this . . ." It was the way he had spoken to the car hop so long ago. Burney saw the tears in my eyes.

133

He did not finish what he was thinking.

"Also, the Law . . . ." He probably calculated my age, which was just nineteen . . . .

Burney stopped pacing. For a long time he looked out the window, through the green tree branches, and along the alley to the spread-out city beyond, to the streets he drove so freely on his days off.

Not out of fear, not out of love exactly, he turned to me.

"Look, Dora. Would you be square with me? And always do the right thing?"

I did not see his face because there were too many tears in my eyes. But I said it, "Yes."

Burney thrust out his good hand. I took his hand in mine—like this—and we shook on it.

If I live to be a hundred, I could never feel more married to anyone than I felt at that moment. There was just a little moment of silence, there beside the sink full of halfwashed dishes. Then Burney took charge.

"You go tell that mother of yours it's all right . . . ."

He faltered just a second, but then he went on in a positive way.

"You tell her we say Sunday. On Sunday we can do the job."

And that Sunday we really did get married in the minister's study, and mother's friends sent some nice banquet flowers, and at home afterwards at the reception all our friends called, and Mrs. McGonigle and others brought silver settings of the same pattern, and two settings of Onieda and—from my Aunt Gee—an electric perc.

Daddy gave us his new Plymouth and one hundred dollars. That evening we went into Chicago and stayed at a nice Loop hotel until Wednesday. We ate in restaurants. We saw five movies. It was just wonderful.

I told Burney again and again that this was a real perfect honeymoon—but I guess he knew that too. Only he couldn't talk about it. Not just yet.

We came back to Haskall, Illinois, very much married—and that was that. In many ways it solved a lot of things. Now I did not need any more schooling. Besides, in my heart, I wanted only one thing: to be a good wife to K.O. Burney and to help us get along. It was my life, and I loved the prospect.

For Burney, it also made a difference. Never before had anyone,

134

in his words, "given a damn about him, just personally." He knew I cared, and that was enough. Besides, he liked the new Plymouth a lot, and though he was too proud to say so, he was impressed by the lovely wedding presents.

In those first days, I found out Burney was not only good, but also a very sensitive person in some ways. Never by word or gesture has he ever mentioned how awful my mother was that day. In fact, he goes out of his way to please her—just as though nothing had happened. I'm very certain mother never told my father anything.

Shortly after the honeymoon, Burney got a single man from Teletek to rent the garage apartment. Through a friend of the McGonigles my mother found us another place, the whole upper floor of a dwelling, "all our own," as she said.

The new place at 231½ really belonged to Mr. McGonigle. We looked at it, but I had no experience with places to live, and had nothing else to suggest. Burney walked through the rooms, and thought a minute, and said, "Right. We're in." For the first time, we moved.

During the first weeks in our new home I came to know what "deepening love" could mean. Not that I pined while Burney was on-shift. I tried to help with little odd jobs, and Burney was pleased when I got full value from our telephone by making calls for a Dance Studio, offering free lessons—a kind of come-on. I used this money to fix up our new apartment. I began with pink curtains in the kitchen, and then made a box spread for our double bed. I bought the paint and painted out the woodwork, one room after the other. Burney was proud of me for doing all of that, especially since I earned the extra money.

Now I think I very probably brought it all on myself.

In redecorating, I finally got around to our living room. 231½ was the upper part of an old house, but in a nice neighborhood. The living room was just awful: flowered wallpaper and a mantel and a fireplace that no longer worked.

First I went to a hardware store demonstration and learned to paint with an antique effect. I began with the mantel, and then did the whole room. In the end, it looked like wood paneling: Old Ivory, with a brushed gold trim that partly followed the moldings. The electrical part was Burney's. He rewired and relocated the lights. It came out just beautiful—and we had done it together.

I did not say so, but now I wouldn't mind at all if people came to see us. Sure enough, some poeple did call. I gave the girls I still knew from my class a morning coffee. They liked our place and said I was a very lucky girl.

"Yes, yes," I told them, and smiled pleasantly, but I would never, never have said what I felt in my heart.

Then Mr. McGonigle happened to drop in.

He was in the neighborhood, and was looking over all his rental properties. He owned this house, and the M&M Furniture Store, and was important in the church where we were married. He was very pleased the way I had taken over. It was very nice, he thought. Actually, had I but called him, why he might have thrown in all the paint from M&M. He smiled, and gave me a large wholesale-price wink.

When Mr. McGonigle saw our new antique "paneling" in the living room, he whistled. "All hard work." Then at the top of the stairs he said, "All *very* good."

We shook hands, and he went on to inspect the other property he owned.

Because he had approved, I was extra shocked to get the letter. It came the next week, not from Mr. McGonigle, but from his Tax Consultant (and Management Advisor). I think it was a kind of form letter, but it stated the point clearly: because of recent increased property taxes for schools, increased interest rates, and Federal taxes, all McGonigle-owned rental property (no exceptions, please) are hereby raised 12 per cent.

I hid the letter, and waited until after our supper to tell Burney.

"Here's something . . . ," I said. "For us. In the mail."

Burney read it twice.

Then he brought his fist down on the table and everything jumped up and fell back and rattled.

"Not right!" and he swore and swore. "Why these improvements. You did them all. Time *and* materials. Why we improved it 30 per cent, why . . . ."

Finally I said perhaps I could handle it. Mr. McGonigle would probably see our place was a legitimate exception, since we had furnished all the materials when—actually—the landlord should have done that.

No. Burney was absolute. I would not bargain or ask any favors. No wife of his would ever have to do that. "Also," and he glared at me for the first time, "You keep your mother out of this."

Burney came back to it.

"Oh, you might know it. Every time. It's us working people who take the old shaft. Every time."

I did not think of us as working people exactly, but I kept silent.

"You know, Burney," I finally said. "It would cost us much more to move than twelve per cent. Over the whole year, twelve per cent would only be . . . ."

"You just watch us," he said bitterly. Again I saw the isolated, lonely side of his character. I had thought being married might change all of that.

"You just watch us go," he said again. Then more reasonably, "We can't let my wages go for rent, year after year. We should save. While we can."

"But couldn't I work? Some? I could do that. And make up the difference?"

"I want you," and it was final, "home when I get here at night. I mean that's what I like most about being married. I want to know I really do support you."

I said, Yes. Yes. He was a man, and my husband. He had to say what we would do on big things. This was our first big decision. Looking ahead, I did not want our decisions any other way. Besides I am not a terribly smart woman, and it is best for us if I am pleasant.

"All right, Burn," and although my heart broke a little, I said very evenly, "you look around for us."

Burney did look around. He came up with—oh, I won't say. It was not nice, but it was something we could better afford. It was up four flights of stairs, in the rear; it was much closer to the center of town, but about the same distance from Burney's work.

So we gave McGonigle notice, and the very first people who came to look rented our place—and the woman laughed at me for leaving all my work behind.

Nevertheless, we moved out on a Saturday.

He rented a two-wheeled trailer. I packed all our new things with care; I helped carry boxes up the four flights of stairs. In spite of the neighbors and the noise, I saw that with some paint our new place might not be too bad.

After the final load, we went back to 231½.

I wanted to take one last look, so I got out of the car, and went up the stairs.

Burney was already in the center of the paneled living room—laughing and laughing.

In his hand was a can of spray paint.

All over the kitchen and bath, and all over our antique ivory and gold paneling, Burney had sprayed great, garish crosses of black paint. Everywhere. Everywhere. Even a big X on the bathroom mirror.

"Now let's see," and Burney's voice came back up the stairs. "Let's see how that bites them."

His voice re-echoing filled each room, and every cleaned-out closet became a mouth—*telling, telling*—the mouths of Mr. McGonigle, and his wife, and the lined-up girls of my high school class—and the loudest of them all, my mother. It was Burney's revenge against them all. In my whole lifetime in all of Haskall, it could never be undone.

That's why I broke down and cried and cried until Burney finally came back and stood for a long time and stared at me.

Then Burney took me by the arm and led me down, down to the parked automobile and the trailer and to all of the new places we would be going all of the days of my life.

God Cares, But Waits

I. *Behind Our Lines*

First the prisoner and his interrogation. Of my final mission into their territory, more later.

Beyond our village the highway crosses a narrow bridge of concrete, and then in a gorge of stone goes north. At four o'clock the subject came pedaling beneath the row of palm trees; I stepped from behind the abutment and grabbed his handlebars. When asked did he "Want a drink of our water," the prisoner's face turned white: I had taken another courier headed north.

Our procedures of Search and Interrogation are prescribed: with the subject facing a wall, legs apart, we search first for the knives or other weapons of offense. Only then may we place our hands first on the crown of their heads, rumpling well the hair, then on the seams of clothing where the saw blades are, then down to the shoes— in his case, rope sandals. Inspection of the body cavities, especially females who wear pads or tampons, takes place at my private office in the abandoned school house. Only after complete inspection may interrogation begin.

Subject courier carried no weapons of offense but when I placed my hands on the crown of his head I noted a soft innocent odor, a coconut-oil pomade. His trousers had neither seams nor fly. When I removed the cycling clips from his ankles, the trousers came apart and exposed completely the lower part of his legs. His "trousers" were only a single piece of cloth, gathered at the waist; the legs were formed very cleverly by use of steel clips. Not until my second interrogation, however, did I see the absolute symmetry of his whole body.

Looking back on that instant of capture, I now wish the prisoner had tried to run. As a CI Captain, long in the field, I do not miss;

as it was, the subject prisoner pushed his bicycle towards my detachment headquarters. The other natives smiled at me pleasantly—a kind of salute; they knew this was planned at Babe Ruth, and besides my previous two hundred and seventeen captures are a matter of informal record in the village. That night the prisoner's interrogation began.

But first a word about my methods. In addition to obtaining military secrets and/or agent-contacts in the Territories, I also take unofficial information for my private files: if subject is married, then admitted infidelities; if single, then deviant sexual practice, relations with Self, and all "chance" encounters. These personal notes I send into the village for "secret" typing and reproduction. In this way I am an indirect moral force in the community.

"You are by profession a *Siziar*"—one who professionally washes the dead.

Subject prisoner declined reply.

I then methodically disclosed other items of his file from Babe Ruth. Our files from Corps Headquarters are very complete and contain, chronologically, all instances of unconscious confession as well as the implications from household wastes; at Babe Ruth our specialists analyze evidence from the field for patterns of conduct and consistent routes of travel.

"Your profession and one living relative—your grandmother—are your excuse to go north. Sixty-eight per cent of the time you go via the bridge—at four o'clock."

Subject prisoner declined reply. I then came back to a phrase he had heard before because I had carefully planted it in his subconscious: "How would you like to drink our water?"

Concerning our water this much should be clearly understood. Although the *Rossiter* or the "Lawyer" may be delegated for morale purposes to the enlisted men, including my detachment barber, I alone—in private—administer all water. One half-gallon in each nostril is often enough. The head fills, rationality departs, and by delicate adjustments the subject is suspended for some hours in a twilight state of full confession. When professionally administered, fatalities are almost unheard of. At that moment the prisoner remained suspiciously calm and so I put my question once again . . . "the water?"

As though to reply, as though to begin his interrogation of *me*— a Captain six years in rank—my subject reached down and took a cycling clip from his right ankle. The cloth fell away from his leg and the light turned his thigh to silver.

Without hesitation, I did the only responsible thing. I kneeled before him, and I forcibly *replaced* the cycle clip around his ankle. I rang for my orderly. Instead of suggesting the prisoner might wish to "Talk with a Lawyer," I ordered this subject held under special guards in a stone cell in our stone outbuildings. I now felt this particular prisoner might be a rewarding exercise, after all.

The next morning, I sent my entire CI Detachment, including the barber, into the field for ten days. I wished to complete this interrogation under Ideal Conditions. When I asked him again if he wanted a drink of our water, the prisoner looked directly into my eyes; everywhere in his face I saw genetic weakness. At that time I disclosed, completely, the secondary information in his file: he had washed the young girl overly long. Why? Consider those unhealthy relations with Self. Why? The light behind my desk shone full into his eyes.

My prisoner did not either reply or change expression. Instead, he bent gracefully and removed both cycle clips from his ankles. It was the flesh of his thigh that glistened and winked and moved like liquid metal in the folds of cloth. For the first time I saw the symmetry of his whole body.

As a matter of command decision, I opened my interrogation drawer. On my desk, I placed a bamboo rod, one end flayed. To my surprise the prisoner neither asked for mercy nor made assertions contrary to our cross-filed data from Babe Ruth. Instead, he took the rod from my desk and somewhat awkwardly—like a girl trying to throw a baseball—flayed the sunlight.

"No. Like this," I said, and brought the "CI Lawyer" down across my own leg. The prisoner's face was ecstatic. Once he saw our correct methods, he went around and around my private office, striking desk and chairs and the plaster walls.

Only after I removed my own shirt and placed myself on the interrogation bench did he see the obligations of continuity. He, himself, cried out as he brought the bamboo "Lawyer" across my flesh. As I had known he would, the prisoner broke down and began to weep. So ended my second interrogation.

Such was the pattern of our next four days: early each morning I suggested our water; in response, the subject removed his cycle clips. Each day I placed a new mode of investigation on the desk;

avidly, he learned our methods. In order, I submitted myself to the knout, the *Rossiter,* the Penis Key, and the Fire Stubbs. Towards the end I even dreamed of the prisoner, head down beside our carboys, a nostril hose swinging in the sunlight like a vine. Still, I held back and so it was, at night, our bodies exhausted, that we began to talk.

"You have told me of your past," he said. "You came from an outlying Province. Because your father was a Tax-Fraud Investigator, your parents often moved. Only your mother is now alive."

On those nights I disclosed secondary information about my childhood: all our white cottages behind picket fences in a hundred villages; helping mother pack china in the barrel of straw for still another move; the ways I kept my teachers morally strong by the little notes addressed to the superintendents of all my old school districts . . . .

As though it were his voice speaking, I heard about my interesting past: recruit days, my medals for services in the Territories as Chief of Patrol; my sought-for commission, my satisfactory advance to Captain, Counter Insurgency. Sometimes his hand lay on my breast and in the darkness of my room we were prisoner and interrogator, almost intimate, almost One. Very much I wanted to administer our water, but this he denied me in the following way.

"Captain," he said on the final night, taking care to speak with appropriate respect. "I will now do the thing within my power." He raised me by the hand and I followed to a room where already he had laid out the ritualistic towels of a *Siziar.*

His insistent hands bathed and bathed me until at three o'clock the telephone beside my bed—my direct line to Babe Ruth—began to ring.

The voice on the wire was Tiger, at Babe Ruth. In code, our Operations Major gave me the co-ordinates of a new transmitter—deep in the Territories to the north. At once I volunteered for this mission. Tiger denied my request. I remonstrated. At last he sensed the urgency in my voice and he agreed I should draw grenades at Dump Two. In less than thirty minutes, crepe-soled scouting sandals on my feet, my body covered by a native *burnoose,* I began my last patrol.

Subject prisoner wept without restraint at my departure. Only once did I look back: from the door of the abandoned school house, his back to the light, he was watching me go. When I returned he would be gone for as a token I had given him my private key to his outbuilding cell. Under formal orders once more, I walked steadily across the valley. At dawn I drew grenades from a watchman at Dump Two, and then crossed easily into their territories to the north.

On the second day, high in the mountains, I crawled beneath bushes and came to the barbed wire surrounding their transmitter. This place was of hard, swept clay, the red and white tower clean and erect in the open space beyond the fence. Beside the tower I saw a house of cinder blocks, with a low, square, green door. Pacing the strict limits of his post, a very large man—a guard— sometimes shouted cadence to himself as he walked. With grenades and the machine pistol held close to my belly, I covered myself with my leaf-colored *burnoose* and waited for dusk.

Shortly past noon I saw the relief guard arrive on the back seat of a motorcycle. To be far behind the lines and to see them talking in their green uniforms and arm bands is always sinister. This new guard was slender, and obviously less military. At once the new guard went into the transmitter house and in the quiet of the afternoon I heard the noise of a toilet flushing.

Finally the new guard returned to the post—with a folded beach chair. The guard leaned the rifle beside the door and unfolded the chair. With the motorcycle now far away, the guard removed first hat, and then blouse. After an almost knowing look around the perimeter fence, the guard took off her brassiere. She reclined in her chair, her face to the sun, her red hair winking in the light. This new guard—a woman—apparently drifted off into sun-bathed sleep.

All afternoon, through a little opening in the briars, I watched the woman "guard" their transmitter. Clearly she was my enemy and yet from time to time she roused herself and peered very innocently, yet very intently, into the hand mirror in her purse. Always before on my patrols I had used explosives, guile, disguise, appeals to pride, or bribery where possible. Now, for reasons I did not understand, I felt beyond Tiger and even Corps; in fact, although I still say our war is Just, I felt beyond the entire chain of our command, both tactically and politically. I began to tremble in my *burnoose,* and yet with grenades and automatic pistol warm near my belly, I forced myself to wait.

What happens next is perhaps strange: some will say I wanted to die, but the fact of my victory proves othrwise. Boldly at dusk, I stood up. I went directly to the main gate: she did not challenge. Therefore I went to the place where she lay. At close range she was much younger than I had imagined. Provocatively—innocently—in the half-light from the transmitter tubes, I saw her teeth and her half-parted lips. For one moment, pistol at full automatic, I stood above her.

Suddenly her eyes opened. Without trying to rise she spoke to me in my mother tongue and she said, "You have come."

In fury I remembered Corps and Tiger. I threw my first grenade. I threw it with great force inside the transmitter. Only then did she cry out. Too late, she saw my face bent very close above her lips.

She cried out again, but I threw my last grenades into the now flaming house. Suddenly, I heard laughter. This was my own voice. I ran across the clearing and leaped the fence and ran down a ravine of stones. I heard the transmitter tower crash down into the clearing somewhere behind me.

I repeat: although the woman guard awoke and positively identified my face, I did not shoot.

On the trails through low jungle to the south, I sometimes wept. Too late I saw my prisoner—now escaped—and the woman guard were in league: what the prisoner began, the woman finished. And it was a fact: I had spared them both.

Therefore imagine my intense joy when I arrived back at the village and crossed the narrow concrete bridge. I found the school house still abandoned—except for my prisoner. He had remained faithful. He had even prepared for my return for food was already on the table. At once I slipped out of my *burnoose* and my sandals and together we ate.

From gratitude and from some apparently deeper understanding, I very willingly taught my prisoner—at last—to administer the water. His confession was lyrical, complete.

Awkwardly at first, then with greater control, he administered the same to me. One half-gallon in each nostril is often enough.

Painfully at first, then in a visionary way, all consciousness left— and then returned. In the end my body outraged by water, I sank again into the isolated darkness of the abandoned school house. Towards dawn, I very clearly heard the prisoner going through the drawers of my interrogation desk taking one of each thing I had taught him—correctly—to use.

Unable to arise, impotent, my Detachment still in the field, I heard the back door slam. The prisoner, after all, was going north. Somewhere this side of the mountain he would meet the woman guard. They would cross-file their notes and together they would view all of the things he had taken from my interrogation desk; together they would go to some house I would never see and there, late at night, they would make their full report. As for myself, I knew well enough what both my sergeant and the barber would report to Tiger and also to Babe Ruth.

Not far up the gorge of stone I heard men counting cadence lustily as they came. I heard my own Detachment march across the narrow concrete bridge and then up the path towards this abandoned school house.

II. *Outside the Cave*

The buildings of the city and of the prison itself were fire under the sky and the land beyond the city's edge with no rain in the past two years was cracked as an old woman's hand: cattle with legs apart in the fence corners, mouths slobbering foam, eyes glazed by the memory of water. In that heat the convict passed walls of stucco where the noise of buckets swinging empty above empty cisterns echoed among the small shops that lay beside the railroad tracks going north across the valley until the rails became a sliver of steel between two hills and then went on into the territories beyond. To himself the convict said, "No. Not yet."

"Going on?" the barber asked and with a white paper bib in place the barber began with the clippers. "*Very* far?"

The convict said nothing for truly he had no plans. Although he had waited years for his release, and although his papers were correct, he now accepted something for the first time: in a coastal city where they had interrogated and arraigned and had tried him, indeed in the whole world, there was no one waiting for him. Years ago his only sister had stood by him for awhile. Now even the judges were dead.

"Shorter than that," the convict ordered the barber, and because he was now free, with good papers, his voice was contemptuous.

"Yes indeed, sir," and the barber went on: so this year not one land owner planted a crop. And to be honest about it, in the whole town only one garden remained green. That one, by rail, twice weekly, got barrels of water marked Salt Cod—it was said. Also:

145

young girls roamed the streets after dark, the government did nothing, and so who was to blame?

The convict in the barber chair said nothing but he heard well enough that girls ran alone in the streets after dark. In the sky overhead he felt some grotesque fowl—all fire—beat its wings.

"Good luck," the barber finally said, and with false enthusiasm whipped off the paper bib. Released prisoners often ducked into his shop like this for they wanted to pay someone to do a personal service, perhaps for the first time in years. The barber resolved to say no more for this one was very pale and very hard and very possibly a murderer—or worse. When the ex-convict looked at him coldly the barber added nervously, "Ahhh, good luck. Ahhh out *there*?"

As the former convict walked along the railroad tracks going north, he happened to look up and see the cave. Because he was going nowhere at all, he climbed the high bank to see about it. This cave was in a ledge of rock and not much larger than his old cell. Inside the cave there was nothing at all; outside the cave's entrance was a large, smooth square of clay.

Because he was fatigued, the convict sat for a while on the square of earth to rest. Towards the town at dusk he saw the lights of the prison workshops suddenly blaze in the heat; along the tracks to the north he saw only the landscape and the rampant heat of the valley flow across the hills like a river.

With no possessions except for the suit of blue serge and the small amount of money they had paid him for work at the stamping machines in the prison, with no very real hope of a future, the convict saw no reason to move on. The money left from the barber shop was not enough for either bribery or a train ticket; therefore he threw all his coins over the bank towards the railroad tracks. He took off the prison-made suit coat and the shoes and placed them behind a rock in the cave. In the old way, exactly at nine o'clock, he slept.

At daylight the convict sat again in the mouth of his cave. For the first time in his life, without rancor, he observed the sun's first rays come up and then spread across the curve of the earth. On the train tracks below the first peasant walked towards the white buildings of the town; past noon a released prisoner in a blue serge suit walked north, eyes on the gravel. No one looked up at the cave in the limestone ledge so the ex-convict who had committed so many crimes against both women and animals did not call down. He watched his morning shadow disappear at noon; he watched his afternoon shadow grow longer and disappear at night when the sun went down.

On the third day the ex-convict slept upright, and awoke to find a youth standing on the square of clay before him.

"Are your lips black because of no water?" was what the boy said, for he was an unemployed drover who had found several coins on the clay bank. One after another these coins had led him upward to this cave. Because the convict had been so long in a cell, he had somewhat lost the habit of speech. He made no reply at all. As a little joke he even pretended not to see the money which the young drover showed him.

From guilt and also from the joy of having found coins that a man in a cave did not claim as his own, the drover boy went at once into the town. At cafes, a little at each place, he spent the money and he recounted his adventure with a black-lipped hermit. Old women begging at tavern doorways heard this story; each one knew in her heart if one coin were found there was always another.

At dawn the convict awoke to see a half-circle of townspeople staring into his blackened, sun-warped face. A beggar woman had found the last of his coins on the clay bank above the tracks; in a respectful voice, she gave thanks. The drover boy stepped forward to ask all of their questions: In fact, had The Hermit been without food *or* water for seven months? Did or did not one melon roll down from the bank above the cave each night and thus sustain him? In what manner were certain of the clay-bank coins changed overnight, in merchant's tills, into gold?

The former convict felt laughter deep in his belly. Once he had been a stone mason but much drink and a vicious temper had caused him to kill a fellow workman. The body had floated many days down a canal, and his first crime was not discovered; after that his violence became more open, and there were others. Finally, almost by chance, he was questioned about a woman's body and the child's body dead beside her. At the trial other things were established. To hear their deferential questions made him feel superior, much in the way his crimes had made him feel beyond the judgment of all men. In addition, he saw one of these "pilgrims" was a young girl with black, serious hair down around her shoulders. The old echoes of desire clanged and clanged in his mind but because he had worked as a mason he thought, "Let's first see how this little job goes . . . ."

With all of the guile and dissimulation he had learned in prison, the convict solemnly raised his right hand, palm outward towards their faces. Well enough he saw the young woman was frightened: this was good for he knew from experience that genuine fright may easily become passion.

As protection against the dust, one man had cloth over his face and so the convict did not at once recognize the barber. As though on official business, the barber walked slowly around the convict: very closely the barber inspected the half-moons of scalp above the ears, the slope of the forehead, the grey-tipped hair growing wildly from each nostril.

"Of course I would know the convict by his neck and his hair. Besides I never forget a customer who tips generously. This man is not the man who came into my shop. I give you my word, this hair was not recently trimmed by a fine barber such as myself."

The first delegation from the town walked back along the railroad tracks and the beggar women followed, making little pods of dust with their sticks.

The convict watched them go and then rolled backward into his cave and laughed until tears came into his eyes. He felt these people were even bigger fools than either wardens or prison guards, themselves always prisoners but because of the pay never admitting it. Nevertheless, to keep up appearances, the prisoner sat again outside his cave and was surprised to see one visitor—beyond any doubt the barber—had donated a few coins. This new money the convict also threw over the bank: others would find it when the sun rose the following day.

Then it began. Beggars and small shop owners who sold cloth and crushed maize walked out along the railroad tracks. They left melons, gourds of water, or coins; each night the convict threw these coins wildly across the landscape for the people who found the money also spread his fame most swiftly to the larger cities where now all canals were dry.

Because train loads of people came early and a great many stayed to imitate the convict's peculiar cross-legged posture or to imitate the way he stared at the landscape, the convict found he could not easily retreat into his cave either to laugh or to take a long, secret drink of gourd water. He saw new respect in their faces. This he had not known as either a prisoner or an honest but violent stone mason; he felt he deserved this attention for none of his trials had been covered well enough by the Press.

Unfortunately, their gifts and coins were in such profusion around his crossed legs he could scarcely move. This effect of opulence distracted his pilgrims from closely inspecting his almost black body and neck and face. In the past week the barber had closed his shop and was now living at the foot of the clay bank beside the tracks. In his loud warden's voice the barber lectured each day's crowds. He told them what to expect when they climbed the bank and also of the miracles: Copper into Gold, and the Profusion of Melons.

On the ninety-sixth day, the convict who now really did look much like a hermit, motioned the young girl to remain beside him for the night. Each day, without fail, she had walked to his cave; he understood she wanted to experience his body for herself.

"Do . . ." and he was surprised at his own voice for he had imagined his first words to her as sounding not coarse, "This, do . . ." and he picked up one coin from the heap and managed to toss it almost to the railroad tracks.

The young girl did likewise. He saw she liked very much to throw the gifts and the melons down upon the barber who suddenly found himself kneeling under a shower of coins.

Desire was what the convict felt, desire clanging in his blood. His hands ached as he thought of the white throat of the girl and of twisting fiercely her black hair around her throat until at the same instant he both defiled her and broke the neck with his remembering, stone-mason hands.

"Place me inside our cave," he said. "Pour all water gourds over my unclothed body."

This the girl did. Then without having to be asked she threw herself on his breast and sobbed, "Yes . . . Yes."

Ironically, the convict now knew his lust was only in his mind. His gulps of water late at night when the barber slept, his fast, the sun all day and the dust, all those things had wasted his body to . . . oh, to crossed sticks which were his legs, to bones that were his thighs, to a protruding, black forehead, to flesh that now seemed almost stone.

She wanted to revive his flesh, but she could only weep in the cave. In his pretension he could only say to her, "Believe, believe."

Then he, himself, was taken by her innocent, smooth-handed desire. To her, yes; but to himself nothing happened.

"But we could," the girl told him softly as she carried him once more to his customary place at the entrance of his cave. "If you will only permit rain to fall. In the valley."

Partly to please her, partly to perpetuate this joke on the herd-minded bourgeois that he so much despised, but most of all for revenge, the convict said it solemnly, one eye on her white throat:

"Rain," he said to the dry moonlight. It was the kind of joke another convict might understand. "Rain. *Comes.*"

After the girl called those words down over the railroad bank, the convict saw the barber running along the tracks towards the town, already making manifest this promised miracle.

Yet in the days which followed the heat overhead beat the entrance of the cave with wings of fire. Now he wore no clothes at all; bleached by the sun, his hair waved across his rutted breast. In his mind he saw what he had become: a thing of influence, his words recorded by the friends of the barber. To men who left much gold where he could see it, the convict passed on a convict's evasive, worldly wisdom; these men of substance used his words to justify business schemes which were both devious and cruel. For this service they left water he could not now drink in gourds of gold.

For two weeks, with longing, he watched the smoke plumes and fire of the railroad trains going across the valley towards the lighted cities on the coast. He thought upon it seriously: he would take only the coins of gold and he would bribe the drover boy to sit in his place for one night. Secretly he would leave this cave and board the train and disappear forever. Yet at summer's end the convict saw it was already too late. And of course he knew: to excuse his own weakness and also to perpetuate the lie of his apparent renunciation of her flesh, impotent and wan, in a moment of sentimentality he had spoken two words and now those words were his ultimate act of deception; to insure the illusion of both simple folk and the prosperous fools, to focus attention on himself, he had promised rain. He felt entangled in the hopeless vines of his own promise. His own words had reduced him to this sack of flesh. His condition was testimony to his own inflexibility and to his own vision of fraud. His days and his nights became one. This was his end.

Oh, he was dying. This comprehension came as both shadow and sunlight when the great wings of heat beat upward without remorse against the cloudless cave of the sky overhead. No rain came and in the delusion of all light the echoes faded inside the cave. Near the end he heard only the monotone of his own blood making the noise of a freight train dying somewhere inside this solitary cell of flesh that was once a man.

For the past week the girl had slept beside him.

In the final hour when he was beyond movement of either lip or hand, he felt a moment of consciousness spring up like the last flame on a hearth place. In that instant he heard a distant sound. He heard it once again. He heard the thunder stamping, heard noise splinter the sky.

He opened his eyes. He saw the girl standing in the cave's mouth, arms upspread, legs apart. In the sky beyond her legs, he saw the great slave whips of lightning lacerate the clouds and the earth. He heard it clearly, heard it across the valley, heard the thousand feet of a running cloudburst: the rain, the . . . r . . . ain.

Half-believing, for a second believing absolutely in himself after all, he knew he was dead, dead and running down the clay bank and across the railroad tracks, running through the downpour into the valley beyond, submitting himself at last to the formal resignation of all landscape.

III *A Transfiguration by Vines*

They awoke in a small valley, a gorge of stones leading down into the town. Beyond the guard rails overhead they heard first an automobile and then two carts on the blacktop road going down; behind and high above on the mountain where once they had camped, they heard the noise of wood choppers at work in the fir trees. The man raised his head. Beneath the guard rails, as always, he saw the road curving away, to reappear at last near a fountain in a green park and go on then into the town below.

The woman turned on her side of their blankets. By raising her head she could also view the place where they sometimes felt they wanted very much to go—at least after long discussions they had agreed once on that point. Now it seemed mostly a matter of time, and the time was not yet.

"Fires," and she tried to take exactly her share of their blankets. Because she was domestic and responsible and hungry she said, "Other women—down there—are at breakfast."

The man took it as a criticism, but did not reply. He was more philosophical and he often thought back to see how it had all begun—so to speak. For a few minutes he looked at the gorge where tiers of young fir trees rose above them, sparkling with moisture in these first minutes of another day. Higher up on the mountain the wood choppers worked steadily in the larger trees.

He threw back his side of the blanket: the vine was still there. He had known it would not go away during the night, but its new growth each day was always shocking. Nevertheless, he was always anxious to see how much it really had grown during the night while they slept.

Yes. This morning really a great deal—as he pointed out to her. Whether this growth was caused by these longer, late-summer days, or by the night's humidity, he could not say. At first he had thought the vine's growth was in relationship to phases of the moon; now he was equally convinced that new growth was related to the water level in the trout stream in the bottom of the gorge. Water, from somewhere, must surely give the vine both food and useful minerals in solution; otherwise, how would the green convoluting vine with its leaves like hammered green metal, tendrils soft as his wife's flesh, continue to grow?

Actually, they had come here in late spring. They had walked down a trail from the melting end of the mountain glacier. When lights of the town seemed very close they had camped in this spot below the guard rails for the night.

The vine, so tiny then, had been there when they awoke. She had intended to throw back their blanket, but he was already sitting upright, examining very intently this small green thing, the first leaf emergent and tender and silly between his great toe and his second toe. He had said, "Fungus," but as they watched, a new tendril curled up and out. By nine o'clock this first new, green leaf was a little bit larger.

"What about stockings?" she had asked, for it was still a few miles to the town, or at least to the green park where the fountain was.

He might have said, "No," or he might have argued that this, too, was a living thing, but he did not; he instead, he accepted it without either fear or discussion. He saw it was without roots and loved the sun and that seemed enough; therefore, they stopped all activity and all future plans in order to contemplate this new, tiny thing which even then was growing larger from between his toes.

Some days he lay with his head on the rucksack, and she lay beside him, and both of them watched his foot and the vine growing. At noon she went to the trout stream and brought back small cups of water to pour over his foot—and also to inspect more closely this new thing which was now really much larger and much more beautiful. Past noon, when the wood cutters stopped chopping, they slept.

Towards nightfall they awoke. She took a little of their food from the rucksack and they ate together. Even after they went to sleep again beneath the stars they felt the vine's newest tendril rustle a little around his ankle and—later—around the calf of his leg. Even in the nights of late summer they did not dream; at dawn they contemplated his new green leg, made green by the vine growing.

At the end of their second month, she realized the vine itself had become his life. This she accepted. His single-minded attention, his hard-minded exclusion of everything else, in fact his adoration of the vine instead of either her or their own relationship made her feel lonely. Once she cried in the night, but he did not awaken. The bad, blue feeling came and she, herself, wished for the green vine to grow inside her belly. But no, and that mood also passed.

Nevertheless, during that night, she recalled a great deal about their old life before this vine came to them: at a place, a town it was in the Territories to the north. They had met when young. What it was like before they met, she did not now care to remember. At first they had gone out at night with other young people in groups; later, alone, they had experimented with drugs and went for long, harmless trips of the "mind"—singly, of course—but still much closer than ever before.

Finally when they were truly together, they had gone into the mountains towards the foot of the glacier. For several days they had camped near beds of wild flowers in bloom—of that much she was certain. Now each day the vine grew a little bit—like a habit—and now it held them both. She did not cry about this anymore and when the tendrils of the vine took his thigh, when she could no longer see all of his body in the old way, she accepted it.

Acceptance, however, was not enough. At times he urged her to leave him, to go on alone into the town. She felt this was neither ultimate affection, nor even mercy on his part for now the roots of the vine had pierced through the blankets and went deeply into the

153

rocks and the soil. If he urged her to leave, it was his way of being a hero; besides, he would have the vine alone and unadulterated for himself. That he could tell her to go on alone made her sad. After all, she had accommodated the vine in their bed from the first day it appeared—innocent and tender—between his toes.

In September, before the rains, the thing finally happened. Deeply, she had wanted it to happen: she awoke but could not get up to serve either him or his vine. During the night, because she had always placed her legs close to his in sleep, the tendrils of the vine had taken her ankles. As they watched, the tendrils ravished her flesh and took her strength as though the vine needed this new thing on which to grow.

When the first rains of fall came down the gorge they did not move for they were both with this vine and—at last—a part of it.

At noon she felt him tremble beside her. What she saw was the first spume of snow, blowing down from the glacier and across the upper rim of the gorge. His breath at noon emerged from his part of the leaves, and she saw his breath turn white against the vine. Worse, the vine itself was now, ever so little, turning to brown.

In fear, in panic, with their rusted camp knife, he began to hack at the vine. When the vine drew back, she saw his neck and his breast. When she saw him again, for the first time in many months, she too began to pull and to cut each tendril frantically. Then each of them got a knife and the vine seemed to pull back and away—but not one tendril withered.

Still, she urged him on. Together they worked at each tendril in order; beginning at the top they pried tendrils from flesh, and did not stop when blood came from each place where the vine had to let go. That night, very late, the first flakes of snow fell in their camp and the vine was almost gone from their bodies.

"Tomorrow," he told her, and she too felt they were free to go. "Tomorrow we will go down into the town."

To her it seemed only an act of the Will, so she put everything she could reach into small piles. Very early in the old way they would get up and pack and go on down the road which they had seen each day all summer. Oh, she knew they were exhausted but she knew they were also together in the old way, before they watched this thing which they had nurtured and had finally accepted and which had, in the end, almost overwhelmed them both. "Good."

And then she added, "I still do." And he answered her and said,

154

"Yes. I still do. I love you."

Then it was morning.

During the night the vine had surrounded them, had grown back tighter than ever before. Now they could not see each other.

Because snow was coming down the side of the mountain very fast, the wood cutters—two of them—doubled-bitted axes over their shoulders, also came down the trails to the road.

That morning the two wood cutters saw this strange thing not far from the guard rails: a vine growing, with great roots going down into the soil. Furthermore, the vine had grown in upon itself—had not climbed either the guard rail or a tree, nor had it run across the rocks of the gorge towards the water, as might be thought natural. More strange than its shape was this: the coiling, triumphant vine seemed to breathe in and out. When the wood choppers placed their wooly ears close to the leaves they heard voices—or something—crying out from the core.

Therefore the wood cutters chopped this very large vine off at its roots. They also chopped away the stray tendrils. With leftover vines they made the whole thing into a long, mummy-like bundle. They also cut down a small fir tree and stripped off the branches to make a carrying pole. With the bundle of vine tied to the pole, they placed the pole on their shoulders. With axes and pole and all they went down the road and around the curves. Whistling as they walked along, the wood cutters soon entered an astonished village.

In that way, riding on a pole, intimate in vines, concealed from the people who watched with much interest as they passed, the man and the woman came to the place they had looked at from afar for a very long time.

In the town square all the following week the children and beggar women and men going home from barber shops or factories on the hill and home from prison or from some army post not far from the frontiers, all of them walked past, and some of them paused for a little while to look. More than one said, "Yes. Something is singing all right, somewhere inside those wrapped-up vines."

And then they walked on.

005810941